Another Son of Man

~ A Novel ~

Tim McLaurin

 Down Home Press, Asheboro, N.C.

ISBN 1-878086-96-0

Library of Congress Control Number
2004107406

Printed in the United States of America

Book design by Beth Hennington

Cover design by Tim Rickard

Down Home Press
PO Box 4126
Asheboro, N.C. 27204

Distributed by:
John F. Blair, Publisher
1406 Plaza Dr.
Winston-Salem, N.C. 27103

We ride the tides of our lives. Some are outer tides pulled by the moon and are visible to us only when we are near the sea or standing outside looking at a full moon. Others are inner tides—our pulse, hunger, sexual appetite, the rhythm of our inner clocks which we feel when we are silent and listening to what our body needs. But all these tides pull us steadily toward the equal plain, the sea, death—that flat playing field where a Rolex has no status over a Timex. There are few variables between two men other than the course they take in getting to that sameness and how they judge their lives when they arrive.

—Tim McLaurin, July 1, 2002, written for an unfinished magazine article 11 days before his death from cancer

Prologue

The translucent chrysalis was dry and empty, its former occupant reborn to flight, the butterfly nowhere in sight. The boy plucked it from a low-hanging tree branch, a momentary curiosity. It was so fragile that he cradled it in his cupped palms.

Higher in the tree, a lime-green bug rested on a leaf, wings shining under a platinum sun. It joined voice with the sing-song chant of brethren kin, one more note to a chorus that washed from tree to tree.

The child shaded his eyes against the glare, but could not spot the singer. He wished he also might fly up to where the breeze tussled leaves, to a place cooler than the stagnant, chafing heat that surrounded him.

The boy's own husk was dry and stretched tight across his bones from lack of food; in sudden fury he curled his fist and crushed the spent shell. Lifting his palm to his face, he inspected the baked fragments of lifeless cells and blew them from his palm. The fragments caught a scant draft and lifted higher and higher above the plain until the boy was only one more darkened spot.

Squat before a meager fire, the woman stirred water while flames licked a blackened pot. From a simmer close to boil, vapors lifted in white curls that smelled of spices plucked fresh from the land. Gnarled black fingers took chunks of goat meat from an earthen bowl and dropped them piece by piece into the seasoned water, the flesh curling in the sudden heat. The woman added chunks of yam and mealy, small potatoes to the stew that had to feed more lives than it should.

Drawn to the scent of the pot, the boy stood naked except for a shirt that brimmed his knees. His belly was round and bold like a pot; his navel protruded like a lid knob. He leaned toward the steam, which mixed with smoke from the fire.

A rooster crowed, jubilant in his dominance of three frowsy hens.

Fingers of vapor and smoke dispersed, rising in a spiral high into the sky above Gabon, joining with dust, flecks of butterfly chrysalis, and billions of water molecules that clotted white against the blue, African sky.

Another afternoon, another supper cloud, the bleating goat's last breath from slaughter knife to stew vapors.

The supper cloud drifted westward to the sea, mixing with like water in transit and hurried by the convection of bright sun upon salt water. The rooster's time for the pot came, evaporation from where the boy peed against the tree — all and such finally sent express at high altitude thousands of miles to the Caribbean Sea where in late summer the ocean was warm. And there, the odors and vapors of inadequate lives began to spin counter-clockwise, like an hour hand turned backwards to the day when the boy's mother, herself a child, stood close to a similar fire and sniffed a meal that also was not enough.

Chapter 1

Trees crowded the shoreline of the lake, looping willows, then taller cypress and red oaks mirrored dark in the water, as two canoes slipped by. Hunkered deep from the weight they carried, the boats were laden with three people and the gear they had chosen to bring. The passengers were not versed in such activity, the crooked path they rowed obvious in the wakes of the canoes. Occasionally one slapped a paddle against water, the noise unusually loud against the curtain sound of late summer insects and frogs. Audible as a cough in church, the broken peace caused a turtle to slide from its log perch, a water snake to drop head first from its coil on a willow branch; a white egret took wing and flew down shore to another blackened knob of wood.

As different as the trees onshore, the people laid their own styles of ineptness into their task. Sitting in the stern, a white man in his late thirties paddled one canoe. In the bow, a slightly older woman of Grecian descent labored. Their canoe was red and sleek and rented. The black man, in his mid-thirties rowed alone, with most of the group's gear stashed in his dented and scarred aluminum craft. The trio traversed Alligator Lake, its water dark with tannin, the preserve linked to civilization only by a pitted, gravel lane that led to a narrow Eastern North Carolina road. Left by the government to the fish and bears, the lake's boundaries bore no houses or private docks, no campgrounds with bath houses, beaches and campfire nature programs; people had to sweat and row by hand to reach such primitive climes. And all to bring to rest a young man's ashes, freed by death from the labor of diseased breath.

Wiping her brow, Ruth peered from under her cap brim at the high sun, her voice loud against the white-noise blanket of nature. "How much farther?" she asked.

"Depends on how fast you paddle," said Junuh Parrot from his seat in the lead canoe. Lifting a cocoa-colored arm, he pointed with his index finger. "See that place where the trees look higher? That's about the only dry land around the lake according to the map."

"That's only about two miles straight across. Why don't we cut across the lake?"

"Too much wind. Besides, we'd miss seeing these sliders and banded water snakes."

"Like I need to," said Reese from his seat in the fancy boat. Thin and sun-browned, taller than his poundage, he lifted his paddle to the length of his arms. "Only good snake is a dead one."

"Where's your sanctity for life?" asked Ruth. "You're a minister. A man of God."

"A snake got all this mess started in the first place."

"Nate liked snakes. He liked everything that comprised life."

"Well, I can forgive him snakes. I've been forgiven for plenty."

Stroke by stroke, the canoes zigzagged. Startled, a great blue heron lifted, heavy wings whumping the air. A turtle raised his head above the surface, then retreated, leaving rings in the water that grew wider and caught the sun with glints of silver. And the frogs sang for rain.

The storm's eye was open now, wide, distinct and round. Calm and blue, the water within the circle frothed with spent energy. Whales and dolphins, the air breathers, sucked in great gulps of air, restoring oxygen depleted cells; fish kept to the depths. A line of clouds swept higher and higher on the horizon; the mammals knew the winds would come again from the opposite direction, waves and lightning to drive them deep with the fish to hold their breath until the sun shone again.

A man studied a radar screen at the National Weather Center. "You better come have a look at this."

Sighing, another man got up from his chair and walked over. Studying the pinwheel shape on the screen three hundred miles off the North Carolina coastline, he raised one eyebrow.

"I thought this was supposed to stay a tropical depression."

"That's what all the indicators showed, but we've got a hurricane now."

"What's the path?"

"Well, we've got variables, but right now it seems to be swinging toward the northern Carolina coast. Hatteras area."

"What do you predict?"

The man frowned, shook his head. "I'd say this storm could come into land in as little as twenty-four hours. Maybe a high-category two."

"You better get it on the horn. Last thing we need is ten thousand vacationers stranded on the Outer Banks."

The paddlers' destination was a hummock of land only a few feet above water level, about an acre in circumference, dry dirt, the trees mostly oak suited to the soil. A sandbar, white against the greenery, separated the lake from dry land.

The canoes were about a hundred yards away, wind fresh to the paddlers' backs, drying sweat and temporarily keeping away the clouds of meddlesome gnats and mosquitoes.

"What are these strings?" Ruth asked as they approached the shore. Every fifty feet hung a length of mason twine tied to the bouncy end of a willow branch.

"Bush hooks," Junuh said. "Someone fishing for catfish. Seems strange, though. You need to check catfish lines every day."

"Why's that strange?"

"There's no access in here except for that small road we drove in on. I can't see someone coming this far three or four days a week to check lines."

A paddle blade banged against the red canoe; the nearest line jerked the bough up and down. Junuh feathered his stroke and brought his boat alongside. The line jerked hard and cut the water. Junuh grasped it and lifted a big, flopping fish into the light and air. Ruth gasped.

"Channel cat," Junuh called out. "'Bout a five pounder. Should I cut it loose?"

"That would be stealing," Reese said. "Some poor redneck is probably making his living off this lake."

Junuh dropped the fish back into the water. His mind floated back years to his brother, Cleo, the time they were paddling Smith Creek down below Charleston and came upon a similar catfish line, and how they had raided it, cut the lines from the branches and brought home so many fish his mother had called over some relatives to help eat them. They didn't have a freezer back then. Remembered his father standing above the boat, eyeing the catch.

"They any tag on the bush? Any name?"

"No sir."

"'Spect they Johnson's lines. He know we fish Smith Creek. He the one I 'spect took our crab pots. A little tit for tat."

"I swear, Daddy," Cleo said. "Won't no names or numbers on the flags."

"Don't swear. And don't do this no mo'." A black man's life to Johnson 'bout as valuable as a catfish."

Junuh's mind left his childhood in South Carolina. "I saw another line moving a ways back," Junuh said. "Yeah, someone's tending this line." Searching the lake, he saw no other craft, only flat water and a brownish-green line of trees, the sky very blue for late August, as if some great sky sweeper had sucked up all the moisture.

Junuh pulled hard on his paddle, and ran his boat well onto shore.

A good site. Dry ground bare of poisonous undergrowth, fine firewood from small cedars that died from the shade of bigger trees. West facing. The sun would hang long over the water. Canada geese would sweep in when the light was low. With morning, the water would hold the mist, and fish would break the surface as they fed. And the humans would debate and decide what time and method was necessary to honor a man's ashes.

Junuh walked the woods and studied the high land, maybe a hundred feet broad and deep, an island, surrounded by a quagmire of shallow water and silt, studded with cypress knees and covered with brier thickets. A compass and machete swamp. Animal scat in the leaves, a raccoon, rabbits, larger black mass dropped by a bear. No worry about bears. The noise this group was making would warn off any animal a mile away.

Junuh stood with his eyes closed, taking in the smell of decaying plants in late summer, mud that bubbled sulphur, lake pungent and sweet and infused with fish. Two hundred miles from the hospital where he worked as an oncologist, the sights and smells and sounds here were as different as the woodpecker is from the catfish. The hospital smelled of old people riddled with disease, making the young people like Nate even harder to accept. For Junuh, once the coo of mourning doves was the sound of morning, but that seemed eons ago. Dying came most often in the hours just before the sun, and bereavement from the people he spoke to in waiting rooms was more likely the first call of dawn, tears from humans replacing the haunting call of birds.

"I've been away too long from all of this," he whispered.

"Dadgum it!" Reese muttered, when his boot got wet as he wrestled a pack-bag from behind the stern seat. "Goddamn it" was on his tongue, but he had left those words behind a few years earlier with the drugs and booze. He unscrewed his canteen lid.

"We must'a done a quarter mile extra from all the zigzagging, Ruth."

"You were steering us. That's why you

15

wanted the back."

Gripping the bow rope, he pulled the craft completely on dry land.

Only yards into the woods, they found an open space the size of a living room. A hole was in the middle of the clearing, probably where some lightning-struck tree had rotted away.

"Mother couldn't have provided for us better," Ruth said. "A natural fire pit, and plenty of room for three tents."

"God the Father, don't you mean?"

"Mother Nature, God the Father, Jesus the Son, Mary the Mother, Allah the Great. Does the name necessarily matter, Reese?"

"The name means everything. That's what you don't understand, Ruth."

Blue veins marbled the woman's temples. "Where was God the Father for Nate? He still died."

"Well, your Mother Nature didn't do anything for him! At least God the Father, through his Son, Jesus, allowed Nate's soul to enter heaven."

"Oh, bullshit, Reese. God is God, and it doesn't have a penis or a vagina. Even a body for that matter. Certainly not a son."

Blue jay scolding. Footsteps in the forest. "Will you two quit arguing?" Junuh said. "I haven't been in the woods for a while. I'd like to hear the birds, instead of two people arguing about senseless things."

"Reese and I may disagree," Ruth said, "but our argument is important."

"I see trees and the sun," Junuh replied. "I'm breathing. In that bag over there is an urn with a young man's ashes in it, and his last request was for the three of us to come into this swamp and disperse them. Right now, that's the only thing that's important to me."

"That's because you're an atheist!" Reese said. "A godless atheist trying to heal people."

"I'm not an atheist, Reverend. I'm agnostic. There is a difference. I just quit trying to understand why a man dies barely in his thirties. Or worse, a child at seven."

"You were his doctor, Junuh."

"And you were his minister, and you, Ruth, were his favorite nurse. We all cared about him, and he still died!"

The discussion was halted by a sudden flurry of sound overhead. A horned owl swooped through the clearing, wings pounding the air, talons briefly gleaming, before disappearing into the trees.

For a moment the only sound came from crickets and the startled breath of the three people. "We have to stop this bickering," said Ruth. "That owl was a sign straight from the universe."

Above the three, another torrent of words filled the air, unheeded by animals, birds and man, a voice spilled from a high antenna in the language of FM. Three short piercing tones, then a long one. A male voice followed: "This is the National Weather Emergency Network. This morning, tropical storm Dena upgraded into a category-two hurricane. It is traveling rapidly toward the North Carolina coast and could touch land within twenty-four hours...."

The voice issued its warning in a frequency too high for humans or the owls to hear, although the owl's more primal ear was already turned eastward, listening to a growing vibration. Too much vibration and the bird would lift wing and fly inland. It knew its layer in the skin of Earth, too much water the boundary of its grave.

The sun followed its steady course across the lake, turning red as it settled behind distant oaks and cypress. Camp was set, tents erected, sleeping pads and bags unfolded. A Coleman lamp was suspended from a branch in a tree; folding chairs surrounded a fire pit where already small flames crackled and popped, the smoke a bug deterrent, no heat needed for late August. Sky clear except for high cirrus clouds that had turned pink from the last rays of the sun.

Food smells permeated the air, out of synch with the redolence of earth, separate pots for different meals, people too varied in their tastes to share the same sup. Reese cooked simplest with a hotdog skewered on a stick. Full hood of night, and everyone had eaten and washed utensils in soapy, boiled lake water. A full night symphony; frogs and crickets, two owls that called and answered, the surge and ebb of katydids and crickets, a whippoorwill that started and stopped and started again.

Ruth, head leaned back, watched stars that appeared much brighter than in the city, a large moon becoming golden through the tree boughs in the east. "Isn't this majestic? I'm so honored to be here. I'm ready to heal the wounds of the world."

"Let's start with Chapel Hill," said Reese. He pushed the baseball cap he always wore back on his forehead.

"Chapel Hill is the healthiest city in North Carolina. It's willing to recognize me for who I am."

"Burlington would recognize you. Then they'd ride you out of town on a rail."

"My God, Reese. You're a minister. Where's your love for mankind?" She tossed her paper plate into the fire. It charred black first, then burst into blue flames. Ruth opened her mouth, curled her tongue. "Do you think you're the only person in this group who's concerned about North Carolina?"

"I bet'cha I'm the only person in this group who was born in North Carolina."

Frog sounds, the fire crackling. An owl hooted as a mosquito hummed close.

See? Like I thought. The only native North Carolinian in the group. The only one to serve in the military." He lowered his voice. "The only one in this group that I know absolutely for sure ain't queer."

Quickly Ruth stood up. "I can't believe that a person as sensitive as Nate wanted you at his memorial service."

Reese tossed a burned stub of hotdog into the fire. "I'm not here by choice. Believe me. He asked me to come say some words, and I said I would. Ain't like he had a church load of kin to attend. He never had a single visitor."

Nate had checked into University of North Carolina Memorial Hospital just two months before his death, already into the late stages of an aggressive form of cancer. He had no insurance. Raised in a series of foster homes, he'd put himself through college, then served as a Peace Corps volunteer in four different countries. He'd been diagnosed shortly after returning to North Carolina. His case had been assigned to Junuh through simple rotation. Ruth had been drawn to his personality, his cheerfulness and simple acceptance of a death sentence. Reese would talk to anyone who listened; so often his spontaneous sermons were met with disdain and ridicule when he started up on a street corner or one of the rock walls on the UNC campus.

Ruth sipped her tea. "No. He didn't have visitors. And he stayed in Africa way past any possibility of curing him. But he always smiled and found something good about his situation. He asked you to come, Reese. He asked me, and he asked Junuh. There's something bigger going on here. I feel it. I've felt it since Nate died."

Junuh lay away from the fire, away from the bickering. He got enough of that at staff meetings. He walked to the sandbar where the reflection from the campfire shimmered on orange ripples. The smell of musk, so different from antiseptics and diseased flesh. Stars punched the night sky — one small and yellowish — Saturn, he remembered. Junuh thought of Nate. Was his soul somewhere between those specks of light, in peace and no longer in pain? If he had a soul? More shouts from the fire. Junuh knew why Reese raged. Reese wanted so badly to believe Nate was now with God, but feared almost as much as he trusted that he twisted in torment in flames. Junuh simply didn't wonder any more. His own brother drowned at sixteen, and despite how he turned that fact, no good sense could be made of the death.

Junuh saw a slow bobbing light along the shore. A single light, diffused and yellow, more like a kerosene lamp than a flashlight. Moon glow on the water? No, the light moved, sometimes stopped for a few moments, then drifted on. The catfish lines we saw earlier. Someone is checking the catfish lines, working them, removing what is hooked, then rebaiting. No motor. Has to be someone staying on the lake.

The light was less than a hundred feet away when Junuh stood. Within the dim glow, he could see the figure of a man sitting in some type of skiff. A circle of light and hands pulling a line, a writhing fish that slung shards of water. Fish unhooked and dropped from the light, two hands threaded the hook through bait and returned the line to the water.

Junuh shouted, "Hello. How's the fishing?"

Circle of light now around the man's

feet. Sound of a paddle as he turned the skiff toward the sandbar. Silently, the boat drew nearer, the man back-paddled and stopped the craft ten feet away. His face in dim light and deep shadows, a beard and long hair, thick lips and a wide nose, eyes blackened, but the man's forehead caught the light and glowed like the moon. He was silent.

"How're you doing?" asked Junuh. "I figured we were the only people camped out here."

No response.

Junuh paused, waiting for the stranger to say something. After a moment he again filled the silence. "I hope we're not ruining your solitude. Sorry for all the debate going on over there."

The stranger inhaled sharply, then spoke in a slow, deliberate manner, as if each word was an effort.

"Debate — a contention by words or arguments. Bicker is one of many synonyms. *First Corinthians* 6:14: 'For ye are yet carnal; for whereas there is among you envying and strife and divisions.'"

Frogs, locusts, the ceaseless whippoor-will sounded, but Junuh remained so silent he could hear his watch ticking.

"There's a big storm coming, Mister," said the stranger. "Much wind. I don't think you can ride it."

Water splashed as he began paddling, backing away from the shoal.

"Wait a minute," Junuh said. "What are you talking about? What storm?"

Only the man's oar spoke as the light

steadily receded.

"WHAT STORM?" Junuh shouted.

The light grew smaller and smaller, only the pulled oar responding.

Junuh's eyes went from the light back to the stars, then to the moon. The bottom half of the orb was covered with clouds. The argument behind him reached a crescendo, followed by silence. Junuh stood for several minutes and watched as the moon was swallowed. Weather coming from the east. Junuh knew weather rarely came from the east. From the forest, an owl embedded his talons into a rabbit. The rabbit squealed. Junuh turned from the lake toward the fire as the stars began to blink out one by one.

Red sparks twisted upon the stiffening breeze. Junuh, mute, took his seat. His mind swirled with the images of the strange man, his deliberate words of coming wind and storms. Junuh extended his legs and intertwined his fingers.

"You look like you've seen a ghost," Ruth said. "What's on your mind, Doctor?"

Junuh chuckled, shaped a smile. "I feel like I saw a ghost. Did either of you see the man on the water I talked to?"

Reese lifted one eyebrow. "Was he walking on it?" He chuckled, a welcome relief from the night's tensions.

"Nothing like that. I'm serious. I talked to a man in a skiff checking the catfish lines. An odd fellow, talked strange."

"He couldn't have talked any stranger

than the conversation that's been going on around this fire. We didn't see anyone."

Ruth nodded. "We were discussing something rather vigorously." She smiled.

Another twist of sparks. Junuh studied the heavens. "There might be a thunderstorm coming. A cloud bank is moving in from the southeast."

Ruth tilted her head, shrugged. "It's not supposed to rain. But some rain might be good. Could lower the humidity."

Junuh shook his head. "I grew up on the coast. I don't like August and storms out of the east."

Reese popped his knuckles one by one. Something big hit the water like a beaver slapping its tail.

"We haven't even discussed Nate yet," Ruth said. "Don't you think we're avoiding the topic?"

Reese hunched one shoulder. "Tomorrow morning we have a little service, toss his ashes on the lake and go home."

"Nate said we would know what to do when we got here. We have to wait for a sign, the answer."

"Nate was on intravenous Dilaudid," Junuh said. "I doubt he knew what he was saying."

Ruth sat forward. "No! Right before he died, he became so lucid. His aura, oh God, his aura was so blue and powerful."

Reese rolled his eyes.

"He was lucid and clear, and he said we would discover what to do when we got here."

"I already know what to do."

Leaning, Ruth squeezed Reese's knee. "That owl that swooped down when we were arguing, that was a sign. We're here for something important. Nate brought us here."

The owl suddenly hooted from nearby, one sudden call that rent the sounds of insects and frogs. "See there," Ruth said. "This is all planned." She stood up, clicked on her flashlight and aimed the beam at the trees. "I have a nature call. Then I'm going to sleep. We should all meditate on Nate tonight. He's right here with us. Just like the air."

Reese pulled a cigarette from his pack and lit it while studying Junuh. "What's up, Doc? You look a little shaken."

"A weird night." He shook his head.

"That's because we're with a weird woman," Reese said in a low voice. "Good in her heart, but too strange for me."

"That guy on the water," Junuh said, "he talked funny. Sounded like a prophet in some old Biblical movie. And these clouds blowing up. Something just doesn't feel right about all of this."

Flickers of twisting light fell upon Reese's face. His eyes reflected the image of fire, face grim. "This whole month has been bad. A storm out of the east doesn't surprise me."

The wind whispered stories in the tree boughs. Ruth's steps announced her return from the woods. "We ought to turn in ourselves," Reese said. "At least rest. I ain't expecting to sleep too good tonight."

Chapter 2

Gray embers, the moon straight up and blinking on and off between rushing clouds. Deep night sounds, a whippoorwill seductive and maddening with repetition, reeds rustling, and the occasional "thunk" from big fish feeding. All going unheard by the three humans sleeping fitfully in padded nylon bags.

Ruth awoke with a start, at first uncertain of her whereabouts. She squinted to see the phosphorescence of her watch dial — 2:15, a long time till dawn. She stared at the reflection of fireflies on the zipped entrance of her tent. Wind in tree branches and that irritating whippoorwill caused her to tense. Wind secrets, could she hear them?

Speak to me, Mother, I am listening. My ears are not tuned to the bedrock, though I cup my ear and lean toward the words. Teach me. I know I am ignorant, but I am eager to learn.

New tent, new air mattress, this cocoon that wraps me, all bought and never tried, no sweat or grime to boast I have come this way before. I have not. Grits and humidity and gnats are not in my breeding. Ain't is not a word. Dixie is only a word, not a history. Reese and Junuh know catfish lines. Their world is just not mine. I would trade the whippoorwill's broken record for one cry of a loon bobbing near the cold shore water of a New England lake. Remember? Oh, I remember so well.

Chilly mornings in late June, school out and that same cottage we went to year after year. The screened window open and through that portal the loon called in singular peals, bell-crisp from the fog-shrouded water, me, under a quilt and fresh from dreams, the lake bird said wake up, it's a new day.

And I could smell coffee and my father's pipe, and knew that he and mother sat at the small table on the porch where they could see the water. They were happy then, or so I thought. At eight I was insulated from unhappiness. But that was many miles away, and years ago. Sometimes I feel old for my years, jaded and cruel enough to want to crush the song from a bird simply because it wants to sing.

Loons. Lonely and singular and unanswered. Sort of like my life. Singular, lonely, liberal, and educated like probably ten thousand other people in Chapel Hill. Give and wait and give and wait. And then those few like Reese. I can tolerate him. Should pity his ignorance. My virtue is to pity and forgive his type. Too busy shouting and condemning to listen; afraid if he opens his ears he might hear words threatening to his beliefs.

Using religion as a fortress.

I wonder if Lynn is sleepless right now. The hum of the air conditioner draped over her frou-frou bedroom, lying on satin sheets, I hope she is lonely and sleepless, and I know I am mean to want that. But I do want it. And I don't want to hear the five-hundredth call of a whippoorwill, or a hick religious fanatic with meanness in his mouth, and I have no idea what Nate saw in his vision and why he wanted us to bring him here. What did Nate see through that window?

"I see circles, Ruth. Circles round and round rising up like a corkscrew, and I am flying except that I can't see my body, but I know I am flying. Something about an alligator and circles. What does an alligator have to do with circles and flying?"

"Medicine will make you dream crazy."

"They're not bad dreams. More like a vision. I can see it right now, Ruth. Through that window. Circles and flying and something big and beautiful just barely out of sight."

Ruth's hands were warm, lightly touching his chest where one of the tumors bulged. Hands full of blood and energy. Ruth could feel the tumor try to roll away, warty and chilly like a toad. If only she might direct that heat and energy better, the beast might hop right out of his chest. She had seen what Reiki could do — black vapor rising from a woman's breast, and the x-ray the next day showing no hint of disease.

"The man you talk about, he wasn't a medical student?"

"No. And he wasn't a dream either. He had the clearest blue eyes, like the sky before the sun rises. And he said I had to go there. He told me the whole reason I was born was to go there. He said life would make sense then."

"And he had a stethoscope?"

"Yeah. And he put it to my forehead. He said that's where the illness is. He said that's where all illness comes from."

Ruth tried to drive the toad from Nate's chest, but it hunkered down and wouldn't move. She felt it, the outline and coldness. "I tell you what, Nate. As soon as you're in a solid remission, we'll go to that lake. We'll go camping there, and in the morning we'll eat pancakes."

Nate was silent for several moments. "I'm not going into remission, Ruth. You know that. Dr. Parrott said the chances are slim."

"Dr. Parrott isn't God."

"I don't have to be in remission to go to the lake, Ruth. You could carry me. I've gotten so skinny, you could carry me on your back. Getting there is important. It doesn't matter how I get there."

Wind in the tree tops. Wind and the endless bird call. At least, through this tent I hear the night and not muted traffic and a clock ticking. New nylon surrounding me, and a whiff of wood smoke when the wind is right, the smell off the lake pungent and fruity. I need prayer.

Spirit Guide, bring me to peace. Take the whirling from my head and let me drift into sleep. Thank you for the sounds of night and this warm bed against your bosom. Let me fall into you and sleep deeply and dream of good things. Thank you for this venture into Mother Nature, for the wind and the frogs and even that bird. May you guide us to understand what Nate wanted us to see. But for now, in this hour of night, might you bring to me pure, peaceful sleep. Amen.

Get my butt right against this air mattress. A white light is engulfing me and filling my body, my mind is floating. The light hums and pulses and blocks the call of the night bird. Go down moon glow and the preying sheet of night. Come sunshine and a better day; I was not born for twilight. Pretty words. Did I make those up? Or are they words passed on to me by another person who tried to make it through a sleepless night?

Junuh cursed silently. Goddamn whippoorwill won't shut up. I was sleeping till he started up again. Can't find the frigging flashlight. Yeah, I was sleeping, 'cause an hour has passed. Wind has gotten stronger. Adjust my shoulders, should have brought an air mattress instead of this celluloid thing. Bird hollering and the tent flapping. Shouldn't be this wind blowing. The forecast was for balmy

August weather, maybe a thunderstorm at worst. I live by what is forecast and true to the model, the dosage of medicine, what prescription to write, some poor soul's life expectancy. The universe is what I can see, smell, taste, hear and feel with my hands. I threw away the words "if" and "should" years ago. "Will" and "did" are so much more appropriate to my life.

Low Country South Carolina is no longer in my universe. Can't see the water or smell the salt, crabs snapping and the sting of sweat. Don't want to — that swampy coastal land is like a book that ought to stay closed, the pictures inside faded and flat. Keep that book closed.

Blue skiff on flat water, Junuh and his older brother, Cleo, pulling crab pots, brown arms bunched with muscles, black eyes intent on what emerged — either food on the table and some change in the pocket or dry beans and the bank man knocking on the door. Feast or famine, pot to pot and year to year.

Wire cage black, wet, shining and dripping, flashes of blue and ivory and a dozen or more crabs that meet the sun with raised claws.

"Hallelujah! Put your trust in the Lord, boys. Like manna from the sky," said Junuh's father, broad-faced and smiling, his sweaty forehead blue-black and shining like a crab's back. "Ain't it, boy? Like manna from the sky."

Gray and white herons standing on one leg in the glades, wind-lace on the water and reeds that whisper as they bend and rub. Skittering crabs emptied into the basket, and the big man baited the cage with chunks of fish. Cleo dumped it, and the rope cut the water, then went straight and taut, his father singing, his long pole pushing the boat toward the next buoy.

"Gotta have faith in the Lord, boys. Ain't gonna let you starve. We feasting off the table of the land."

Unpainted house with oyster-shell yard, chickens pecking for bugs. Thunder grumbling from dark clouds in the west. Junuh's mama reading from a book while Cleo begged to take the boat out.

"Them pots hold a few more crabs. You ain't going on that water alone."

"Can't sell drowned crabs, Mama."

"Better them drowned than you. Your daddy be up and about in a couple of days. You sit there and rest and listen to this story."

And like an omen she read a story of a man bitten by a mad dog while swimming in a hurricane flood. That's mighty bad luck, she says.

Drowning in a hurricane flood. In a hurricane flood. Drowning....

Flicking on his watch light, Junuh closed flat the picture book in his mind and sent Cleo back to the deep water, his parents to that year of the hurricane flood. He squinted his eyes hard, but they were dry. He stared at the black ceiling of his tent. I should have heeded the warning right then, but I'd have had to tote Mama hollering and beating my back to higher ground. She wasn't leaving without him, and Daddy wouldn't have left if riders on horses mounted the clouds. Would have drowned with a mad dog before he would have left without Cleo.

Cleo. Died sucking down salt water. And Nate died in his bed, his lungs filled with liquid. Not so different. Two deaths about as necessary as a mad dog swimming in flood water. I had to see Nate's eyes, stark, searching and trusting, chained to the bed with IVs. At least Cleo died free. On his decision and free. Nate was all mine. And me with a shortage on "should" and a stockpile of "will."

Deep breath at the door of the room, fluorescent light shone on the back of the patient's bald head. Junuh held his breath and stepped forward, like plunging into frigid water.

"Hey Nate. What are you drawing?"

On an art pad against raised knees, he had sketched in colorful ink a meadow scene.

"I'm drawing where I want to be. Outside. Ruth says I ought to use image therapy." A butterfly IV was taped to the back of his hand, plastic line stretching from vein to suspended bag of clear fluid.

Leaning, Junuh studied the picture. Flowers and butterflies, birds in the air, a bright sun. An alligator lay on the bank of a lake. "That's a happy looking world you have there, Nate."

"It's heaven. That's where Preacher Turner said I was going to be soon." Nate stared at his drawing, kept his eyes from the doctor's face.

"There are alligators in heaven?"

"Alligators aren't bad," he said, looking more intently at his drawing. "I've dreamed of alligators lately."

Taking his stethoscope from his gown pocket, Junuh listened to the man's heart and lungs, told him to raise his arms and take deep breaths. The sounds of dark waters, of streams and growths beyond the healing warmth of sunlight.

"When am I going to die, Dr. Parrot?"

"Who said anything about dying?"

"Preacher Turner said we're all going to die someday, but that my time is going to be a little sooner."

A sudden rage in Junuh's heart, not that the preacher was wrong, but that he was so honest and so right. Yet the preacher did not count the possibility of "what if," and "what if" should be an option. "We're all going to die some day. That's true. But no one knows his time. You may outlive Preacher Turner."

Looking up from his drawing, straight into the doctor's eyes, Nate asked, "Do you really think so?" His blue eyes were especially stark with no lashes or brows to soften them.

"I hope so, Nate. I truly hope so. You're a lot more pleasant to be around than

Preacher Turner."

Nate stared with vacant eyes toward the window. "That man came to visit me again last night."

"He did?"

"I woke up in the middle of the night, and there he was standing by the bed."

"What did he say?"

"He didn't say anything. He smiled and showed me a necklace he wore."

"What sort of necklace?"

"It was a real cool necklace. He had half of a seashell on a strip of leather. On the inside of the shell were stars. They shone and twinkled just like those in the sky."

"I think you were dreaming, Nate."

"It wasn't a dream. It was real. Real stars, too. I looked into that shell and felt like I was falling into it. Like I used to feel when I was a kid and would lie on my back and look into the night sky."

"How many times has this guy been to visit you, Nate?"

"That was the third time. I must have fallen asleep. I was looking at the stars, and all of a sudden it was like I was waking up, and the man was gone."

Junuh wrote some numbers and notes on the chart before hanging it at the foot of Nate's bed. He patted his thin leg, then left the room and walked across the hallway to a large window with a good view of the hills to the east. He took another long breath, then exhaled slowly, letting the wind whistle between his lips. Thought about stars and summer nights when he was a boy lying on his back looking deep into the heavens. Remembered his canoe at home, an old aluminum Coleman he had salvaged years ago from the home place. Recalled being in a canoe with a paddle in his hand, air that smelled of fish and decaying leaves, the sun warm on his face. For a moment, Junuh wished he could pray for Nate, but he had given that up years ago.

And I would pray now if I thought the words would be heard above the wind that whips the branches outside, distinct syllables listened to by an intellect who could quieten the blow. I no longer try to intervene. A sleazy businessman living to be ninety, or a innocent child dying at birth, neither any longer seems to be caused by adhering to a particular set of rules. I don't disbelieve, I just no longer try to comprehend. I'll play by the rules because rules are needed, but I don't believe any longer that a fair game helps ensure winning. If I did, Nate would still be alive, Mama would still be reading Zora Neale Hurston books on the front porch, and outside of this tent right now, stars would be shining.

A cigarette. Maybe another cigarette will stop this freight train rumbling through my head. The good Lord has delivered me from the booze and from the dope, but he's taking his time with the cigarettes. Nicotine has me hooked like a fish. But, I'll lick it one day. Forgive me, Lord, but I need that smoke right now. Out here in the middle of the woods with a nigger and a queer — Reese caught himself — forgive me, oh Lord, for my weaknesses and sins, but out here in the boondocks with a black atheist and a homosexual tree hugger, Lord, I need a smoke. I am weak, and I need a smoke.

Reese clicked on his flashlight, found his hard-pack and lighter in the corner of the tent and fired up a Marlboro. He listened to the wind. Blowing steady and sometimes in big gusts. No rain yet. Hadn't rained a drop. Hoped rain was falling at home. The garden needed a good watering, especially the tomatoes. Hoped it didn't rain here. This craziness is uncomfortable enough without mud to slide around in. Wind blowing pretty hard for no rain. A gush of blue smoke in the flashlight beam.

Reese was a conservative voice crying in the liberal wilderness of Chapel Hill. He had founded a campus fellowship for Christians at UNC, and often preached in the brickyard during the lunch hour where he was usually heckled by students.

He followed the newspaper and television news and often spoke at public forums during town council meetings about issues that concerned or confronted his religious beliefs. He was a regular at the area hospitals where he concentrated on terminal cases, trying to get the patient's soul in line for heaven. Somehow, he managed to put in forty hours a week as assistant meat manager at Harris Teeter Supermarket.

Reese wiggled on the foam pad. Too thin. He wished he had a good ol' rubber bitch like they'd used in the Army. Four inches of air. He knew sooner or later he'd fall asleep. Probably later. But, as with all adversities in life, this whole ordeal had to be for some good. That was God's plan. Everything in life was the good of the Master's plan, even if that good isn't apparent at times. Reese believed that. He had to.

In the rose garden outside the entrance to the hospital, Reese dropped to his knees, surrounded by fragrant white and pink flowers. He stared into the deep folds of a white rose, trying to blot out the sounds of traffic, of footsteps on concrete as people came and left through the big glass doors. He was a rough-cut man with mutton-chop sideburns, handsome in a cheap way like a B-grade Elvis.

Reese fingered the plain gold cross that hung from a chain around his neck. Moving his eyes from the rose petals, he fixed his gaze on a clearing in the sky where the blue heavens were deep and stark between a cleft in the billowing summer clouds.

"Dear Lord God and Savior," he began in prayer, "thank you, most gracious Father, for this day and your many blessings, for the gift of salvation given to us through the shedding of Jesus' blood. I ask for your strength and guidance as I go into this building of suffering. I ask for the right words to say to this man who is so ill. I ask that you strip the disease from his flesh, that he be cleansed in

Jesus' blood, that most importantly he be washed of his sins, so no matter the number of days he has left on this earth he finds his reward in heaven. In the name of Jesus Christ, I pray. Amen."

Slowly Reese stood. He brushed the knees of his pants, then turned and marched toward the doors of the hospital into a lobby that looked more like that of a hotel than an institution of healing. He rode the elevator to the sixth floor, straightened his tie, and took a couple of deep breaths outside the patient's room. He tapped on the partially closed door, then stuck his head inside. He saw Nate lying against his pillows, his face turned toward the narrow window.

"Hey, Nate. You care for a little company?"

Nate turned his face from the window, his eyes dark and hollow. He smiled, drew his legs up and wrapped them with his arms. "Hello, Preacher Turner." His voice was weak.

Reese shook his friend's hand, then settled into a chair beside his bed. "Anybody been to visit today?"

Nate nodded. "Ruth was on duty this morning. She said she'd be back after work tonight."

"How you feeling?"

"Pretty good. Dr. Parrot has me on a new pain medication. It makes me a little sleepy, though."

Reese thought about sleep for a moment. Most nights for him were long hours of rolling from back to stomach, fragmented dreams, focusing his eyes on the luminous

clock face to realize that only thirty minutes
had lapsed since the last time he looked. Pain
medication? A man of Nate's age shouldn't
know any more about pain control than what
was needed to ease the throb of a stubbed
toe, maybe at worst a sprained ankle from
playing pickup hoops with a group of friends.
He shouldn't be hooked intravenously to a
vial of liquid Diluadid, a drug that street junk-
ies shelled out thirty dollars for a four milli-
gram tablet that was melted in a spoon with
water above the flame of a cigarette lighter,
pulled up into a syringe, then pumped into a
vein. A big, orange pumpkin exploded behind their eyes, then hours in the toll-free
zone. Reese still remembered that golden
rush, although it had been a long time since
he last jammed a needle in his arm.

Nate's eyes went back to the window.
"What's the weather like out there?"

"Hot and sticky. Hurricane weather."

"I wish I was outside. I'd like to fly a
kite in a hurricane," Nate said. "I bet you
could get it up pretty high."

Reese chuckled. "Might fly you away.
There's some powerful wind in a hurricane."

"I'd do it," Nate said. "I wouldn't care
if it blew me away. Maybe I would come down
in Kansas."

Reese thought of The Wizard of Oz, of
Dorothy and her dog sucked up into a land
where all of a person's wishes were already
granted; they only had to realize that fact.
"Wish in one hand and spit in the other and
see which one fills up first," he remembered
his father always saying. If his father was

drinking, he usually substituted shit for spit.

"When am I going to find the good in this?" Nate asked. "You said there was always something good in anything bad that happens."

Reese hesitated. He didn't really have an answer. "Sometimes the good is hard to see. But it's there. Sometimes you just have to look hard."

"Ruth was crying when she left this morning. She tried to hide it, but I knew she was crying. I haven't seen the good yet. Sometimes I can't help but wonder if there really is any good."

"Blow against your palm," Reese said.

Nate cocked his head.

"Hold your palm up and blow against it."

Lifting his hand, Nate blew against the base of his fingers.

"Feel that?" Reese asked.

"I felt air against my skin."

"You couldn't see it, though."

"No."

"That's sort of the same thing as faith. You feel it, even if you don't see it with your eyes."

"I made my breath. Why can't I just make myself well?"

"God can make you well. You just have to believe hard enough."

"I believe hard as I can."

"Believe it stronger than a hurricane. Believe that it can pick you up and take you away, then set you back down as gently as if you were riding in God's palm."

Nate nodded. "The mountain man

came to see me last night."

"Why do you think he comes from the mountains?"

"Because of how he dresses. He has long hair and a beard, too."

"He could be from Franklin Street. A lot of long hair and funny clothes there." Nate and Reese both chuckled.

"I asked him where he lives, and he said at the top of the earth."

"Maybe he's Santa Claus."

"I'm too old to believe in Santa."

"But not too old to believe in mountain men who fly in the window."

"I didn't say he flies in the window. He's just in the room, and then he isn't."

Reese touched the bag of pain killer slowly dripping into the boy's blood. He recalled the drugs he'd done, the hallucinations he'd seen when he got real bad. Maybe the mountain man was Jesus.

Reese wondered if he was the only one in the group not sleeping. But being here is for a purpose. As much as he hated to agree with anything Ruth said, he had to admit he shared her adherence that all things in life were for an ultimate good. Reese knew that, just as he knew the wind whistles through the branches when the night should be calm, and that he, a former drunk and dope addict, was alive when a trusting young man was now only ashes. God's plan didn't have to make sense to Reese. He was mortal, and God's plan was immortal. One day, with his feet in the water of the River Jordan, Reese knew he would understand.

Chapter 3

Silence, no coo of mourning doves. Junuh knew instantly something was wrong about the day. Late dawn, weak light through a thick cloud cover. Cooing doves were the dominant image of morning for Junuh, stretching back to when he was a child. First light in summer through the open bedroom window, he awoke to song birds twittering and doves calling, that lonesome sound that made time stop. Junuh heard no doves now, not even song birds, only the low and steady murmur of the wind.

Glancing at his watch, Junuh knew the sun was above the horizon. Normally, he would be driving to the hospital now to begin his morning rounds. His head would be full of patients and problems, but at stop lights he sometimes heard doves from their perches amid islands of trees surrounded by the carnage of development. Where now were the doves and the birds and the white haze of an early August morning?

Junuh unzipped his sleeping bag and sat up. Reborn into the morning feet first, he scooted from the tent, his knees creaking as he stood erect. He scanned the camp and saw the other two tent screens zippered shut. The gray ashes from the fire the night before were banked against one side of the pit where the wind had blown them. He reached back into the tent and retrieved his sneakers and shirt. He wondered if Reese and Ruth had slept better than himself.

Junuh sniffed cigarette smoke, glanced around, and saw Reese sitting in his chair on the sandbar at the water's edge. He wished for a hot cup of coffee. The sky was dark and low, the fire ashes pocked with craters where splatters of rain had fallen. After leaning and tying his shoes, Junuh walked toward Reese.

"Morning, Reese. I hope you slept better than I did."

Reese's cheeks hollowed as he drew air, then relaxed as he released a blue stream. "Hey Doc. I don't know if I slept at all. The wind blowing all night."

"Yeah, I can't figure out this weather." Junuh unzipped his trousers and began to urinate in the water. He glanced over his shoulder toward Ruth's tent. "I ain't bothering your morning meditations, am I?"

"Prayers," Reese replied. "We're not in Chapel Hill."

"Prayers, then. I hope I'm not disturbing you."

"Naw. It ain't like I got to disconnect or anything. The line remains open between me and the Lord."

"What does the Lord say about this weather? The forecast was for clear skies."

Reese sucked once more on his cigarette, then threw the butt into the lake. "He hasn't commented. Kind'a worries me, though. Steady wind out of the east. Month of August. You get my drift?"

At a sudden gust, Junuh's stream of urine blew backward onto his leg. He cursed, and turned sideways to the wind. "Yeah, I get your drift. I grew up south of Charleston. I know all about wind on the water."

"So, what do you propose we do, Doc?"

Junuh zipped back up, then brushed a few droplets from his trouser leg. "We sure can't turn on a television. I guess just wait and see what happens. Hope some kind of front is passing through. Keep your line open to the Lord."

"That line stays open. What about your own line?"

Junuh watched ripples on the water. "I disconnected my line a few years back. I didn't feel I was getting my money's worth."

"We need to talk about that. An atheist doctor scares me."

"I never said anything about not believing. I just don't try to understand any longer."

"An agnostic doctor scares me, too." Reese looked from the water to Junuh. "You could be God's instrument. Kids and young adults ought not to die from cancer."

"They ought not die at all," Junah said. "And if there was a benevolent God, kids wouldn't get cancer in the first place. Old people wouldn't either. I just don't try to understand any longer."

Reese held his tongue, but looked skyward and prayed silently, *Jesus, show him the clear path.*

Junuh turned his face toward the gusting wind, the waves kicking up on the lake, and his mind retreated to that day in the low country of South Carolina.

Sunset was upon the water, the reed thickets like stalks of dried corn, the sky dappled with high clouds turning pink, then red. Junuh shaded his eyes with his palm as he searched the far shoreline for the boat and his brother. Cleo should have been back hours ago, and now that darkness was setting in, Junuh's stomach had begun to twist. "Please God," he whispered. "Let Cleo be all right. Please bring him home safely."

He heard steps behind him on the dock, and turned to see his mother.

"What you looking at, Son? This sunset is mighty pretty."

"Just looking, Mama."

"Supper be ready in a minute. Where's Cleo?"

Hesitation. Junuh's mouth hung open. If he would just see the bow of that skiff round the bend where the channel flowed into the broad bay; Cleo had been wearing a red tee-shirt when he left and the color would show like a buoy. Twilight was settling fast, and the glow on the reeds fading.

"Where's Cleo, Junuh? He out in the boat?"

He turned slowly, his eyes on the deck,

then to his mother's face. "Cleo went to pull pots, Mama. He left about mid-morning."

She seemed to age in that moment, the lines on her face deepened, the gray in her hair just a bit more. "He should'a been back hours ago. That boy knows he ain't to pull pots by himself."

"Maybe he had a big haul. They ain't been checked in three days."

Going down to her knees, right there on the rough, salt-faded planks, she turned her face to the painted sky. "Lord, let him be safe. Bring him home safe before the dark comes in."

Despite his bad back, Junuh's daddy and two of his uncles went looking for Cleo an hour later. The tide was down, and they found the skiff blown up on an exposed oyster bed. The catch box was nearly full of blue crabs, but Cleo wasn't in the boat. In the early morning hours, Junuh heard his mama praying where she lay across the couch.

Ruth heated another pot of water. She positioned the stove so the windshield blocked the breeze, then made green tea and sweetened it with honey. With the tea, she had granola with soy milk. Reese had instant black coffee and a can of Vienna sausages in barbecue sauce. Ruth listened to the banter between the men. No one seemed to have slept well. Ruth surely hadn't. Had strange dreams all night, kept thinking she heard breathing outside her tent. Had to have been the wind.

• • •

White light through the window and just seconds later the thunder boomed; the glass that her night-time water was in rattled against the saucer. Ruth was ten years old and a big girl now according to her parents; they allowed her to stay up till eleven on weekend nights. But the light through the window came quicker, more brilliant, the thunder like some great fist slammed against a table, and she slipped from her bed and hurried down the hallway to her parents' room.

"Daddy," she said, touching his shoulder. He mumbled and rolled to her. Within seconds she was beneath the covers between the warm bodies of her parents, her father's big hand upon her shoulder. She didn't jump when the next lightning bolt blazed the window and the thunder was almost one with the light. The rain started then, and she was sleeping soundly when the thunder grew rumbly and long as the storm moved east from the lake toward town.

Ruth saw the man when he was still several yards away. He came from the sandbar where a boat had been pulled up. Her eyes widened as he approached.

"Looks like we have company," she said in a low voice.

Junuh leaned and spoke to Reese. "That's the man I talked to last night."

Reese stood. One of his hands was

curled into a fist. "How you doing, Mister? Glad for you to join us."

Ruth put down her cup of tea. Even in Chapel Hill, this man would stand out. He was of medium height with the physical features of one who probably had bi-racial parents — intense blue eyes above a flat nose and wide lips, light skin, but his shoulder-length hair was a tangle of black dreadlocks. He wore only sandals and knee-length trousers with a tattered blue shirt. Around his neck was a leather strap that disappeared beneath his shirt. He stopped a few yards from the group and stood, turning his eyes from face to face.

"How's the catfishing?" Junuh asked. "We spoke last night when you were checking your lines."

The man did not answer. Junuh glanced at Reese. Although to Ruth the man was bizarre in appearance, he did not seem threatening. In fact, in his clear eyes she sensed a peace and awareness she saw in only a very few people. She immediately wanted to have a conversation with the man.

"Would you like some tea?" Ruth asked. "This water is beginning to boil."

"Tea," the man repeated. "*Webster's*, an infusion of leaves used either medicinally or as a beverage. The twentieth letter of the alphabet. A small mound or peg on which a golf ball is placed before the beginning of play on a hole. I've never played golf, but I have drunk tea. No thank you."

Ruth stared at the man, momentarily taken aback by his response. "Well, if you change your mind, I have some green tea here that is very good."

"Do you live here on the lake?" Junuh asked.

"Live. *Webster's.* To be alive; have the life of a plant or animal. I live in paradise."

Reese arched one eyebrow as he studied the man. "Paradise? What sort of paradise?"

The man stood awkwardly erect, his arms stiff by his side. Paradise. *Roget's Thesaurus.* Arcadia, ballpark, bliss, cloud nine, delight, divine abode, Eden. There are more words."

"You live in Eden?" Reese asked.

"Paradise." The man turned slightly to his left and pointed toward the lake.

"My name is Ruth. What's your name, if I'm not being too bold?"

"Son."

"S-u-n, or s-o-n?" Reese asked.

"Son. *Webster's.* A male offspring. The second person of the Trinity."

Reese cocked his head and stared at Junuh. "You are the Son from paradise. I guess you're a carpenter, too?"

Son shook his head.

"What do you want from us?" Reese asked.

Son pointed at the cloudy sky. "Come with me to paradise."

"What for?" Reese asked.

"Come with me to paradise," he said again.

The members of the group migrated closer, spooked by the words of the man.

"This paradise," Ruth said, "Why should we come with you?"

Son pointed at the sky again. "*Job* 1:13: 'And behold a great wind came across the wilderness and struck the four corners of the house, and it fell among the young people and they are dead.'" He pointed at the sky again. "Come with me to paradise."

Reese stepped close to Junuh. "Is this guy a nut, or what?" he whispered.

"I think he's autistic," Junuh replied.

"What in the heck is he talking about?"

"Sounds like he's trying to warn us. I am worried about this weather." Junuh held his hand up toward the man. "This wind you're talking about. What do you mean?"

"Hurricane. *Webster's.* A tropical cyclone with winds of seventy-four miles per hour or greater. Hurricane Carter's real name was Rubin. He was framed for murder. Paradise is safe from hurricanes and murder."

The man turned toward his boat and waved with his arm for people to follow. Everyone exchanged looks, eyes wide, confused.

"He's a nut," Reese said.

"I like him," Ruth responded.

At his boat, the man turned and beckoned again. When no one moved, he got into the craft and pushed away from shore. The group watched silently as he rowed out of sight.

"What a loony," said Reese, breaking the silence.

"What was that talk about hurricanes?" Ruth asked. "This wind hasn't stopped since last night."

"He's a nut," Reese repeated. "Son of the Trinity. Wants to take us to paradise. He might be dangerous."

"He's obviously autistic. That hurricane talk scares me, though. I wish we could flip on Greg Fishel for the morning weather on Channel Five."

Reese kicked the knob of a protruding root. Thunder had sounded, each rumble a little shorter and closer. "What about a radio?"

"Yeah, I wish we had a radio, too. Anything that gave the weather."

Reese kicked the root again. "We do."

"Reese!" Ruth cried. "You know we weren't supposed to bring any modern conveniences except camping gear. We agreed on that."

"Look, I have trouble sleeping. Aren't you glad now that I brought it?"

"We're not here to keep tabs..."

"Get the radio," Junuh interrupted. "Let's try to tune in some weather."

Reese thrust his head and shoulders into his tent and emerged with a portable radio the size of his hand. Junuh took it from him, turned it on and removed the earphone wire. Country music erupted, then static, as Junuh turned the dial. Rock and roll, more country music, rap, he stopped suddenly as he passed a voice and turned back. A man was speaking.

"...The eye of Hurricane Dena is approximately seventy-five miles off Morehead City with sustained winds of ninety-seven miles per hour. Hurricane-force winds are already reported at Cape Lookout. The storm and is expected to sweep through the extreme eastern counties this afternoon before veering back out to sea along the Virginia line. Residents along its path are urged to take precautions."

The group listened in stunned silence. "That's coming right toward us," Junuh said. "We should have followed that guy."

"To paradise?" Reese replied. "I believe in heaven, but I'm not ready to go there."

Junuh fetched a map and studied it. "Damn storm is going to pass right over us, probably in the next three or four hours. We couldn't row off this lake in three hours. Not with this kind of wind."

"What do we do?" Ruth asked. "We should have gone with Son."

"With a lunatic?"

A sudden burst of lightning turned the world white and was followed by a deafening clap of thunder. Rain began falling. Junuh folded the map and stared at Reese. "You're former military, Reese. We're fixing to be under fire. What would you do?"

"Pray."

"I don't pray."

"Dig a fox hole. If a hurricane is coming, stuff is going to be flying like bullets. Doesn't matter, low as this land is, we'll probably drown, anyway."

Ruth felt a sudden, inappropriate thrill. For most of her adult life, she had read about adventure. She sensed now that she was about to truly live. She took the urn containing Nate's ashes from the pack and sat it where she could see it.

At the highest point from the water, the three took turns digging with the folding military surplus shovel Reese had brought. The ground was soft, but filled with roots that made the work slow. The canoes were dragged several yards on shore and turned upside-down. The hole was about three feet deep and big enough to accomodate them.

Weather seemed to explode. Rain fell in sheets and lightning flashed almost continually. The smaller trees bent against the wind.

Everyone piled into the hole, Ruth between the men, packed tight and lying low. Each had stuffed items they deemed especially valuable into their shirts. Junuh carried the radio and a first-aid kit. Ruth had her arms clasped around the urn. Reese had only a copy of the *King James Bible*. He began to quote verses aloud.

As the wind increased and the day blackened even more, the rain fell so hard that the hole began filling with water. The three hunkered figures shifted and turned in discomfort, fearing dangers outside the hole more than their unspoken fear of drowning in a pit of their own labors. Around them, the wind shrieked and cried, the rain stinging the flesh. Flying debris kept the three hunkered in their watery bed. Large tree branches tumbled past, and they could hear huge trees giving up their resistance and crashing in the darkness. Throughout the fray, Reese continued to pray, at times his open mouth silent against the sounds of devastation around them.

Despite her discomfort and terror, Ruth felt an exhilaration she had never experienced. She realized that all of her days had been spent insulated from the dangerous aspects of life. She clinched the urn to her bosom even tighter. In this moment, with the wind screaming and the white electricity scalding the air, she savored each breath, felt immense gratitude when a tree cracked and fell in a place not on top of her. She was alive in this moment, and all that truly mattered was this moment, a joy she hadn't known since childhood.

Ruth's father never ate breakfast, just guzzled cup after cup of coffee. He was already outside getting the boat and fishing equipment ready. As Ruth finished her pancakes, an occasional loon still called from the lake. Her mother sipped tea as she filled the wicker picnic basket for lunch — deviled eggs, fried chicken, macaroni salad and ripe tomatoes. A quart jar had been filled with KOOL-AID and ice, then wrapped with newspaper and an outer layer of aluminum foil. Her mother hummed as she worked, making sure she had packed all the essentials, napkins and flatware, salt, pepper and a garbage bag for the trash.

The second week of their annual vacation at the lake cottage had just begun, the days in which all the knots and kinks that came from a school year dissolved, and the clock slowed — days especially long and lazy.

Ruth's father drank less during that second week, usually only beer, as if the tension he carried had dissipated. Her mother hummed more often and sometimes sang.

"You two need to hurry along," her father said from the door. "The fish will quit biting before long."

Ruth quickly ate the last bite of pancake and carried her plate to the dishwasher. Minutes later they were on the water, her father's arm muscles flexing as he rowed, Ruth and her mother together on the front seat where they were less likely to get splashed. The lake was still foggy, but the sun was gradually burning it away. Ruth saw dark knobs as turtles stuck their heads through the surface, could sometimes hear fish jump.

Her father threw out the anchor at a spot where, he said, big rocks hunkered under the water and fish liked to hide. He baited Ruth's hook with a worm, then her mother's hook. He didn't fish on this trip. He fished early, leaving as the sun was rising, always taking a fly rod and dry flies — something Ruth didn't understand, but she knew that was how the long fish with sweet flesh got on her supper plate, the nights when her father talked about how the fish tail-walked. He drank a lot then, and usually went to sleep early in the recliner.

Ruth stuck the cane pole out from the boat and swung her line away. The hooked worm sank until the cigar-shaped bobber went vertical. Maybe a minute passed before the first perch struck, the bobber jerked several times at first, then went under, and the line began to cut across the surface. Ruth jerked so hard that the small fish flipped into the air and landed flapping in her lap. She squealed, as her father grabbed for the fish.

"You don't have to jerk so hard," he complained. "Just lift the end of the pole."

"It might get away."

"God, you've got the line tangled now."

"She's just a child, Ron."

"She doesn't have to break the fish's neck."

"Fish don't have necks, daddy."

That was how the mornings usually went on the annual fishing trip, Ruth and her mother catching maybe a dozen yellow perch and blue-gill keepers, once in a while a trout that was unusually stupid, according to her father. That night, Ruth's mother would fry the fish until the tails were crispy – Ruth's favorite part, and they would eat the smoking flesh with cole slaw and French fried potatoes covered with catsup.

"Why was that trout stupid, daddy?"

"Trout are smart fish, honey. They won't usually eat worms on a hook. It takes a lot of expertise to catch a trout."

"I don't need expertise. I just need a worm to catch fish."

Ruth's mother laughed. "That's right, Baby. We don't need a thousand dollars of equipment to catch fish. And they taste just as good."

"Women don't understand trout fishing. It's like going to church."

Ruth, her mother and father went to

early mass every Sunday morning when they were home. Ruth could see no similarity between mass and fishing, except that you were supposed to be quiet.

Ruth's mother was unpacking the picnic basket when she covered her eyes with her hands. "Everything looks so bright."

"You want my sunglasses?"

She shook her head, then a moment later pitched forward into the water. The doctor later told Ruth and her father that the aneurysm had killed her almost instantly, that she had felt no pain. The priest told Ruth that the brightness her mother described had been angels coming for her.

Reese felt the hair on his back tingle and knew lightning was very close. He molded himself against the earth, praying, then heard a *zzziiiiip*, and the world was instantaneously white, followed by a boom so loud that his ears seemed to stop working. He tasted copper in his mouth and knew that once again the Lord had spared them. Reese had known a similar sound, had felt it more than heard it. He remembered exactly what he was doing the first time it came to him.

Eating a MRE, Reese sat on top of the Abrams turret. His luck was bad. He had drawn what they called beans and balls, the main course a glutinous container of white beans and meat balls in some type of tomato sauce that tasted as bad as it looked. He held a meat ball up on the tines of his plastic fork.

"You could catch catfish with this stuff. The worse it smells, the better a catfish likes it."

Zzziiiip.

"I've seen catfish eat..."

Zzziiiip. The meatball exploded, and as Reese's brow was creasing, the sound waves from the first sniper shot reached him. CRACK! Real sound, not the burp of split air, and Reese could not fall backward fast enough. Zzziiiip. A flicker of fire danced off the turret, and the rifle's crack came well behind the projectile. Suddenly, men were shouting and racing to action. The turret turned toward a brown hill, and the fifty-cal began to spit out bullets that the sniper perceived as zzziiiips until the gun's sound reached him — if he still had ears to hear.

That's how close the lightning was at times. Reese could take bites out of the wind-driven rain, and punch it with his fist. He shouted scripture, swore at the Devil.

Junuh moved and spoke the least, keeping his eyes closed and his teeth gritted. He had to turn his face away from the wind to breathe. He had large nostrils and the horizontal sheets of rain threatened to drown him. Junuh knew that one of the stereotypical ideas about black men was that they couldn't swim. Can't swim and like to eat watermelon and are especially afraid of snakes. Junuh could swim, but he was afraid of snakes, and as a child, loved a good ripe watermelon with salt sprinkled on the crimson flesh. Today, he didn't eat watermelon in public. Rarely ate fried chicken in public, either. Junuh had deserted his color years earlier on that day he left the sprawling, unpainted house with the oyster shell yard, rocking chairs on the front porch and stacks of crab cages on the dock.

Junuh went with his daddy to the morgue. He remembered the white paper tag wired to his brother's toe, his whole foot protruding from beneath the sheet. Junuh's heart was pounding, and when the man flipped back the sheet, Junuh had his eyes squinted so he couldn't see well. His daddy's sharp inhale, then the long, steady out-breath.

"That him?" the white man asked.

"That's my son."

Junuh had opened his eyes enough that he could see his brother now, but what he saw wasn't his brother. Bloated, the skin stretched so tight he resembled a doughboy. Didn't look like Cleo. The natural color had even been washed from him.

"What we got to do to get him home?" his daddy asked.

"Sign some papers."

"Why it take so long to call us? You say he been here two weeks!"

"I'm sorry, Mr. Parrot. He had no identification. If you hadn't called, we might..."

I called five times. Described him. Told the lady what clothes he was wearing."

"I know, but..."

"But he was black, and y'all get a plenty of drowned niggers down here. We all look alike."

"I'm not saying that, Mr..."

"You don't need to say it. I know it."

Junuh looked once more at his brother — or at that discolored, swollen lump of flesh, and he remembered Cleo as he waved at him from the skiff.

"He be more proud of me than mad," Cleo had said. "Time he slowed down anyway. Me, I man enough to pull pots alone. Won't hurt my back. Won't have to listen to him tell me what I do wrong, either."

Cleo waved again when he was well upon the water, and Junuh wished he had gotten in the skiff anyway, against his brother's wishes. Cleo was wearing a red University of South Carolina Game Cock tee-shirt, and Junuh saw that spot of fire until the boat rounded the far bend.

Junuh had his mouth open, heaving for air like a grounded catfish. He didn't eat catfish anymore, trash fish born for poor folk — those smoking-hot filets, crunchy with corn meal, served up with hushpuppies. Instead, Junuh now ate tuna steaks, the outside seared, the middle still red and barely warm. Bottom-fish eater or sushi connoisseur, he was mammal and needed air to breathe, and right now he wasn't sure if there would be air enough to breathe, or if he might end up in the depths himself, food for catfish.

• • •

When the storm finally abated, Reese emerged first from the tangle of tree branches and debris that had covered the water-filled hole. Muddy and dripping, he turned in a slow circle, mouth agape at the sight before him. The campsite was no more, the tents gone along with their contents. He spied the ripped material of one tent hanging in a tree. Limbs were down everywhere. Trees had fallen, some snapped off at the trunk, others pulled up with the roots. Junuh helped Ruth up before pulling himself from the hole.

Everyone, they discovered, had been injured in some way, though not seriously. Reese had a nasty scrape on one shoulder. Ruth had an egg-sized swelling on her head and was shivering violently. The temperature had fallen twenty degrees.

The rented canoe had disappeared, carried away by the wind. Junuh's aluminum one was wrapped around a tree trunk, one side split to the keel. Of the more than ample four-day stock of food the group had brought, only two flat cans of Reese's sardines in mustard sauce were still in the fire pit, where they had stashed food and cooking gear. All the freeze-dried and instant foods were scattered through the swamp.

"Let's spread out and look," Junuh advised. "There's got to be more stuff out in the brush."

Thirty minutes of struggling through the torn undergrowth produced only one soggy sleeping bag and Reese's canvas knapsack, open and containing only a jar of instant Maxwell House coffee and two cans of Vienna sausages. Ruth found the pewter goblet she had brought, but not of the bottle of good wine she had hoped to enjoy at sunset by the shore. The level of the lake had risen, and most of the sandbar was under water.

Fortunately, Junuh had kept the radio dry in a stuff sack inside his shirt. He clicked it on and was glad to hear the hum of static. "I imagine most of the power is out around here."

Toward the low end of the dial, he picked up an NPR station. A man was speaking about the storm's co-ordinates. "Reports of damage and widespread flooding are coming from throughout northeastern North Carolina," he said. "Thousands of customers are without electricity, according to power company officials, and emergency crews are being brought in from other areas."

Ruth couldn't stop shivering.

"We ought to get these wet clothes off and try to dry them before it gets dark," Junah said.

"We ought to be getting off this lake before it gets dark," Reese said.

"It took us three hours to paddle in. Now we have to walk, and who knows how long that might take? I say we dry our clothes, build a big fire tonight, and start out at sunrise. At least, we have plenty of firewood."

"All of it wet," Reese muttered, as the three began to strip down to underwear.

In a cubicle at the National Weather

Service, a man sat in front of a computer screen with three colleagues standing behind him. The hurricane was distinct and shaped like a spiral nebula with a hole punched in the center, resembling a child's pinwheel.

"She's stopped," the man said. "Dead in the water. She's sitting there pulling in moisture and getting stronger by the hour."

"She ought to be barreling out to sea," a woman said.

"Ought to. But that's not what's happening."

"What are we looking at?" another man asked.

"God only knows right now. She could turn back inland. One thing I'm pretty sure of is that she's not going to downgrade. She's sitting over the Gulf Stream gaining strength."

The man at the computer typed in a command. An area of the coastline to the north and south of the storm was highlighted in red. "Let's get out the alert. This could become a category-three storm. Maybe a four."

The woman walked to her own desk, picked up the phone, and began to punch in numbers.

Chapter 4

As silently as fog upon the water, Son's skiff appeared at the edge of the sandbar. He ran the bow of the boat aground, then stepped onto the sand. Ruth saw him first and instinctively crossed her arms over her bra. "Look who's here. It's the swamp man."

Son swung his head from side to side as he approached, his eyes taking in the damage from the storm. He carried a bucket in one hand. Ruth looked at her bra, then back at the man, as if she had decided to stay with her near nakedness.

Reese studied the man. Son wore the same clothes as earlier that day. His face carried little expression, eyes like flat pools of water, as if half-naked people in the middle of hurricane destruction did not faze him. The campers migrated closer, and again Son stopped several yards from them.

"Hey fellow," Reese said. "You seem to have survived the storm okay."

"His name is Son," Ruth said.

"Yeah, Son," Reese replied. "You and your boat seem to be in pretty good shape.

We didn't fare too well."

"F-a-i-r," Son replied. "Pleasing to the eye or mind, especially because of fresh, charming or flawless quality." His eyes went to the sky, brightening. "F-a-r-e, the price charged to transport a person."

"Well, I'd say right now we're more interested in the second definition," Reese replied. "What would you charge to get us off this lake?"

Reese's mind was churning. The man's skiff would carry four people. They could all be off the water by nightfall. Even if his truck was damaged, they could walk to civilization. He patted his back pocket and felt the heft of the new wallet he had bought recently. "I'll give you twenty bucks to take us off the lake."

"B-u-c-k," Son spelled. "A male animal, especially a deer or antelope." The momentary sheen of his eyes disappeared. "What do I need twenty bucks for? I only can eat one at a time."

"Dollars," Reese snapped. "I'll double it. Forty DOLLARS if you'll help us get back to the landing."

Son stared at Reese, his eyes flat again. He extended his arm with the bucket.

"What's in the bucket, wild man?"

"Jerky, venison. From a buck, not dollars. *Exodus* 16:15: 'And Moses said to them, It is the bread of which the Lord has given you to eat.'"

"Jerky is not manna," Reese said. "And how do you know so much about the *Bible*?"

Son pointed toward his boat. "I'll take you to paradise."

Reese felt a chill roll up his back. "We need to get to my truck."

"Paradise," the man said again. After a moment, he put the bucket on the ground, then turned and walked back to the sandbar. "It's not far away."

"I think we should go with him," Ruth said.

"Are you nuts?" Reese said. "Paradise?"

"He's dry and clean. Whatever paradise is, it's obviously better than here."

"He might be dangerous," Reese said. "He looks dangerous."

"He's the most peaceful soul I've met in years," Ruth said. "His aura extends about ten feet."

"His odor extends about ten feet, too," Reese said.

Son stood in his skiff for several more moments. Leaning over, he took a tin pail, scooped water from the bottom, and poured it over the side.

"His boat is damaged," Junuh said.

Son then pushed off into deep water. He was soon out of sight as soundlessly as he'd arrived.

"Spooky," Reese said. His lips moved silently as he said a prayer.

Junuh had been taking in everything. He stepped to the bucket, picked out a piece of jerky, smelled it, then took a tentative nibble.

"You're going to give yourself food poisoning, Junuh," Ruth said.

"I think this stuff is safe," Junuh replied. "This guy obviously has been living off the land for a while."

"Probably some survivalist type," Reese said. "An anti-social freak."

"I don't think so," Junuh responded. "He seems concerned about us. I wonder if he lives alone."

"He spooks me," Reese said. "Always quoting the *Bible*. Defining words. Looks like a wild man."

"John the Baptist quoted the *Bible* and looked like a wild man," Ruth said.

"Yeah, and that was two thousand years ago," Reese replied. "The dress code has changed."

"Did you notice his eyes?" Ruth asked.

"What about them?"

"The color and shape. Such a deep shade of blue. Reminded me of Nate's."

"They're just blue," replied Reese. "Lots of people have blue eyes."

The scarlet sunset set the lake ablaze. Birds had returned from their refuges, doves cooing, songbirds twittering. Owls, too, were back. Rainwater continued to drain into the lake until at dusk the sandbar was under water. The group had re-clothed themselves and gathered a large pile of wood to fend off the night.

"No insect repellant or tents, the mosquitoes will eat us alive without a fire," Junuh said.

Reese coaxed a small fire for several minutes, blowing on it to keep the flames alive. He slowly added sticks until he had enough red embers that he was sure the fire would continue. "What I wouldn't give for a can of charcoal starter."

"A true camper doesn't need anything but two dry sticks to start a fire," Ruth said.

"How many times have you rubbed two sticks together?" asked Reese.

"Well, I haven't, but I don't claim to be a camper. If I did, I'd rub sticks together like Daniel Boone."

"Daniel Boone used gun powder and flint. When you've walked all day and scalped Indians, you don't want to fu--, uh, I mean, mess with starting a fire."

Darkness was settling, the air thin compared to the heaviness of the evening before. The sounds of night were beginning. Ruth had found one of their cooking pots in the woods, and was heating lake water in it. One chair had been recovered, and the men let Ruth sit in it. Reese circulated a can of Viennas, each person eating a couple. The goblet was passed with steaming, instant coffee. The jerky remained in the bucket.

"Going to be a long night," Reese said. "The air is gonna be full of mosquitoes."

"They might all be blown away," Junuh said. "The lake sure didn't blow away, though. It's fuller."

"I noticed the sandbar is gone," Ruth said.

"I believe the water is a foot deeper," Junuh continued. All these creeks and marshes draining into it. It's going to be hell trying to walk out tomorrow."

"We'll leave at dawn," Reese said. "We sure can't stay here."

Ruth stared into the small flames.

"There's something to all of this. More than just bad luck. We all were close to Nate. He asked us to bring his ashes here. Not the ocean or mountains — here. Son, the swamp man. Have any of you noticed his resemblance to the man that Nate talked about?"

"Don't start that crap," Reese said.

"What about the man?"

"This guy's just an idiot back-woodsman. Ain't that what you said, Doc?"

"What I said was I think he's autistic," Junuh replied. "Not an idiot. Often people with autism are very bright. They just don't behave in conventional ways. Some are savants, brilliant at particular things, music, for example, or memorizing the dictionary, or the *Bible*."

Junuh looked over at Ruth. "Ruth's right. He does resemble the man in Nate's vision. It's sort of spooky."

"Ah, crap," Reese said. "You two will be seeing the bogeyman in the dark by nightfall." He began to tune the radio. A blast of rock and roll filled the air.

"Tune it to nine-fifty-five," Junuh said. "That's where we've been getting weather."

A woman's voice gushed from the speaker. "Now stationary, the eye is fully defined and the storm seems to be gaining strength. We now have joining us Milton Clark of the National Weather Service. Mr. Clark, what do you think this storm is going to do?"

"Debra, we have a different kind of storm here, an unusual scenario. In another twenty-four hours, it could be a category-four, an intensity not seen around here since

Hurricane Hugo devastated the South Carolina shoreline in 1989.

"Right now the hurricane is like a child's top with people blowing on it from all directions. As long as everyone keeps blowing, the top will remain where it is. But when someone stops blowing, the top will go in that direction. And right now, the three directions are out to sea, up the Atlantic coastline, or back inland — right over the land she passed the first time."

"But this time as a category-four, instead of barely a category-two?"

"That's right, Debra. The worst scenario is if she turns back over land, especially over the areas already wrecked and flooded by her first pass."

Reese clicked the radio off.

"Not listening won't make the hurricane disappear," Junuh complained.

"We better start praying the storm goes out to sea, instead of listening to the radio," Reese grumbled.

"I've seen what your praying accomplishes," Junuh snapped.

"Yeah? Well I've also seen what your medicine heals," Reese said, his voice quickening.

"Stop arguing," Ruth pleaded. "Arguing is the last thing that will help us. We have to help ourselves out here. Don't you two understand that?"

Chapter 5

Wisps of clouds raced north across the moon, as if the storm were a vacuum sucking toward her eye. Except for an hourly update from the radio, the three people ignored the weather and watched the fire, feeding it scraps of wood, a continual effort with fuel wet and green. Remarkably, the sounds of night animals were not deterred by the storm. A lone whippoorwill began its mournful cry about midnight and called without ceasing. Owls argued close by, causing the humans to feed more sticks into the fire. Little conversation ensued, each person alone with deep thoughts and fleet, shallow dreams.

Ruth and her lover were kissing deeply, the mounting passion prompting them to grind their pelvises together. As Ruth felt an orgasm mounting, she woke from fragile sleep. She opened her eyes in time to see a glowing stick crack in the flames, red sparks issuing from the fracture. Ruth's loins felt warm and aroused. She touched her hand to the top of her jeans, wished she were alone in bed and could masturbate.

Rain fell the day that Ruth's mother was buried in her pre-paid plot in Green Meadows Cemetery. Ruth remembered the old saying that rain on a funeral meant the angels were crying. She took that as a sign that her mother was in heaven.

Ruth and her father gradually stopped going to the lake house. It was too haunted with memories, the curtains her mother had made, the worn chair under the lamp by the window where she read when rain fell. Ruth tried to tend to the flowers her mother had planted in the raised beds, but rain fell often that summer, and bugs and weeds stayed ahead of her. For a couple of months, the child in her refused to admit that her mother was gone; she kept expecting to wake up from a bad dream, or for the door to open and her mother to come in carrying grocery bags. The lake house was put up for sale at the end of that summer.

Ruth forked the gray lump, her stomach refusing to let her mouth accept it.

"It's meat loaf, baby," her father said. "I made it special because I know it's one of your favorites."

"It doesn't look like meat loaf."

"I used the same recipe. Just give it a taste."

Ruth took a small bite just to please her father. Nothing tasted the same as when her mother had made it, not the oatmeal or the grilled cheese sandwiches. He didn't even try to make desserts. She chewed the bite of food, feeling the wad swell larger and larger in her mouth until Ruth knew she would choke if she didn't spit it out. She spat, then laid her forehead against the table and began to cry in great, heaving sobs. Her father came to her and wrapped his arms around her.

"I miss her, too, baby. I miss the way she made meat loaf and her laugh and the way she smelled. I know you miss her, darling. Only time will make things better. But you'll see. It's me and you. We're still a family."

Three years later to the month, Ruth stood again in the cemetery, watching her father being laid to rest following a brief but fierce struggle with a brain tumor. She was numb with grief. This time she didn't envision heaven and angels and golden streets. She refused to pray to a God cruel enough to take both her parents so early. A man patted her shoulder as the casket was lowered into the ground, her mother's brother. She would now live with this uncle and aunt.

"This isn't really your room, it's mine," her cousin told her every time they got into an argument. "I'm just letting you stay here because you have no place else to go."

The next four years were a sort of hell for Ruth. Her aunt and uncle tried to be kind, but inwardly they resented having another child to raise, another mouth to feed. That emotion showed in small ways.

"Your cousin is right, Ruth," her aunt said. "Do I have to put a stripe down the middle of the floor? You need to keep your stuff on your side of the room. There's barely enough space in that bedroom for two girls as it is."

Ruth had seen the check that came each month from her trust fund, but little of the money seemed to go directly toward things she needed as a teenager.

"I don't care what's popular at school. This sweater fit Jennifer just fine last year and you're not too good to wear it."

The family attended a conservative church that opposed dancing, rock-and-roll music, and most other things that young people liked. Ruth had few friends, fewer dates, and her resentment grew. She lost her virginity during the first week of college, more out of rebellion than her desire for the boy she barely knew.

Is that all it is? she lay thinking later that night. The earth didn't shake; I really didn't enjoy it. She lay with a damp washrag between her legs to catch the sticky goo he had filled her with. During that first year of college, Ruth drank whiskey and beer, smoked pot, and slept with five more boys. The first time she smoked pot, she remembered laughing at first, but then having intense feelings about her dead parents that left her huddled and weeping. Her GPA at the end of the first year prompted her to attend summer school to improve her standing, but she went more to stay out of her aunt and uncle's house than to excel. She did graduate — in three years due to summer school — and though she received no honors, she got a diploma.

After graduation, she married Jerry, whom she had met in history class. Jerry had been wonderful in the beginning. Even though his college degree had been in business, he elected to work in a bicycle shop; they often went camping on weekends, smoked pot, and watched sunsets. Jerry knew the names of constellations and could point out planets. But after three years of marriage, he sold the bicycle shop, accepted a managerial position with East Coast Cycles, cut his hair, and started wearing suits to work. The marriage lasted only another year.

After her divorce, Ruth drifted for a while, eventually ending up in a commune in Maine, an experience that weaned her from middle-class America. Stephen, the spiritual leader, demanded complete obedience, doled out food and drugs, and chose who slept with whom. But not thinking or choosing felt good to Ruth for a change. She might have stayed at the commune, but Stephen disappeared one day with all the money and dope.

With Stephen gone and no one to direct their lives, Ruth and the other commune members drifted away one by one. In addition to giving her the secrets of baking good whole wheat bread and the pleasures of sex with another woman, life in the commune also had introduced Ruth to Reiki, a form of energy healing. She was attracted to its mysticism and the nurturing nature of its practitioners. She wanted to give to others in ways *her aunt and uncle had failed with her. She decided to go to nursing school, and in her spare hours, to take classes in alternative healing.*

Between studying medical books and mystical texts, she worked on centering herself. She had spent so many years letting others define her and guide her life that she wasn't sure who she was. She had no use for a God who would take her parents so early, so she investigated many religions, borrowing bits and pieces she liked, until she was comfortable with her own form of spirituality. Words like He and Father were left out. In fact, men in general played less and less a role in her life. Occasionally, she would go out with a man, and sleep with him if she found him attractive and nice enough, but more and more frequently it was women she wanted to be with. Not until nursing school did she have her first true female lover. That relationship had lasted seven months, and when it ended, the pain and loss she felt were much more intense than when her marriage had dissolved.

So, here Ruth was, entering middle age, divorced, openly bi-sexual, a Mother Nature freak and vegetarian with long, black graying hair and a flexible, toned body she kept fit through yoga. She loved Chapel Hill and the freedom she felt there to be herself. That was the only love Ruth felt anymore. When she was honest, on sleepless nights, she admitted sometimes that she had loved no one since she had kissed her father's forehead just before his heart monitor stopped beep-

ing. Loving simply provided too great a potential for being hurt.

Some creature cried from the forest, sounding like a baby.

"Bobcat," Junuh said. He folded his arms against his chest. Reese stirred the orange ashes, tossed another piece of wood onto them.

"Could be that swamp man howling."

"Don't talk ridiculous," Ruth said.

"He looked like he could howl."

Ruth's eyes stayed on the fire.

A baby. When she was truthful, that was what she wanted most in the world, a child of her own, her likeness to live after her spirit had departed, to pass on to another child, and that child unto another. Immortality in a sense. A baby had not come from the loins of men she did not love and barely liked. Even more frustrating, a baby had not come by way of four artificial inseminations. She had converted the sperm donors' credentials and statistics into fantasies. Height, weight, race and IQ she combined with her own to create a child. The fourth time, her period had been only two days late when she peed into a cup and waited for the plus or minus sign to appear. She had cried for an hour.

She believed in a benevolent God, but she often wondered about all the pain in the world. Why was she denied a baby when she so desperately wanted to bring life into this world and protect, love, and keep it from pain. She fervently believed there was a plan, a reason for everything — she would go insane otherwise — but why couldn't she fathom it?

She remembered Nate's eyes, large and dark, the ventilator down his throat capping his words, as on a sheet of paper he drew spirals over and over with a pencil. He pointed at the spirals, then passed his flat palm down his body and motioned at the sky. "Inside the circle, I will return to you," he had written on the paper. Again and again he had gone through the routine in his last hours. Trusting blue eyes and a machine that chugged and breathed for him. Inside the circle, I will return to you.

Everything in the universe is a circle, Ruth thought. Dawn to dusk, season to season, tide to tide. Which circle was Nate talking about?

Sweat from the heat of the fire formed on Junuh's face, but the smoke from the green wood kept most of the mosquitoes at bay. Still, occasionally he had to slap his neck, though Ruth frowned when he did. I've tried to please white people too long, he thought. A bug is a bug. The moon moved through the ripped tree tops, but Junuh knew the night would be long and mostly sleepless, and that tomorrow would be a test of mind control. He was good at mind control — willing the hand or foot to move even when the brain says let it rest. He had walked his way out of worse quagmires, coastal South Carolina one of them.

That white, white letter in a rusty mail box. That white, white paper, folded three times. He only had to read the first line to know the door out had opened for him. "We are pleased to inform you that...." The letter did not say he now had the chance to move beyond color, but a part of him knew that was its unspoken message. It was a pass from his past, from being judged by skin pigment.

"Oh, praise the Lord," his mother had said. "A blessing from the Lord." She fluttered her hand and made the white paper flap like a wing.

"I'm not sure I'm going, Mama."

"'Course you're going! A fool let a chance like this slip by. Paid for and all. Praise the good Lord, I knew I was doing right, reading them books to you since you old enough to hear. Knowledge. Poor ol' Job had to pay so much to learn it, but they gon' pay you, child. 'It cannot be gotten for gold, neither shall silver be weighed for the price thereof.'" She hugged Junuh. "Job sitting in ash cloth and sores learned this, and you going off in a coat and tie."

When his father came in from the crab pots, he read the letter slowly and nodded, but didn't speak. In the aging man's eyes, Junuh saw his three older sisters who all had married and moved away from the marsh-land. He also saw Cleo's reflection on that fateful afternoon when the sheet had been pulled back and he was bloated and gray from salt water.

"I can become a doctor, Daddy, have the money to move you and Mama away from here."

"Away from what? The tide and the wind and the water? What else in the world is there? 'Let the sea roar, and the fullness thereof; the world, and they that dwell within.' This is the world, boy."

On his very first day at UNC, Junuh was overwhelmed by the difference from the world he knew. White girls talked with black boys. He had a teacher who not only was black, but talked with a British accent. Nobody called him boy, neither was he ordered about by white people. In fact, most of the whites he encountered seemed especially polite to him, almost nervous to be in his presence. Only rarely did he hear the word 'nigger' and that usually was from other black students. Even they were different from people back home. Many were on the athletic teams and stayed in their tight little groups. Some were loud in class, seemed to want to draw attention to themselves, and Junah's natural reserve caused him to withdraw from them.

"We're having a rally at the pit tomorrow at lunch," a black girl told him as they were leaving class during his freshman year. "Can we plan on your support?"

"A rally for what?"

She cocked her head. "For the inequity of black instructors at UNC. Didn't you read the BSJ last week?"

"What's the BSJ?"

"Where you from, nigger?"

Junuh recoiled at her words. "From South Carolina. Down below Charleston."

"Well, you're not in South Carolina now. Better get the cotton out of your ears."

Junuh attended the rally, but stayed on the fringes. More whites were talking into the microphone than blacks.

Throughout most of his undergraduate years, Junuh stayed to himself. He had few friends and so little extra money that he only went home on holidays and in the summer. And when he did go home, his father seemed gruffer, the house older, and the inlet he had fished for so many years not nearly as broad and blue. His reclusion and focus on studies earned him a 4.0 GPA and admission to the UNC Medical School.

Exams had ended, and Junuh went with some friends to dinner. One of the girls suggested Claydon's, a popular restaurant near Durham that featured Southern country cooking and was owned and operated by a black family.

"You'll feel like you're back home," Sarah said. "I love this place."

After being seated, Junuh noticed he was the only black customer in the packed restaurant. As soon as he opened the menu, he recognized all the food, collards to pork chops; the house specialties list included chitlins. The prices were double what he would have paid at a restaurant back home.

Fifteen minutes passed before the tall black woman came to take their orders. She seemed bored.

"What are chitlins?" one of the students asked.

The waitress propped her hand against her hip. "If you don't know, you probably won't like them."

"What are they, Junuh?"

Junuh's face flushed. "Hog intestines."

"Hog guts!" The boy slapped the table. "Ma'am, bring me a helping of hog guts."

Most of the group ordered catfish. Junuh ordered meat loaf with mashed potatoes and black-eyed peas. Meat loaf was the cheapest entree.

Twenty more minutes passed and the food still hadn't come. "They're sort of slow here, aren't they?" Junuh commented.

The guy who had ordered the chitt'lings laughed. "Junuh, you've been in Chapel Hill too long. We're on black time here. It's slower. They probably had to chase down the pig."

Junuh didn't laugh. When the food finally arrived, the waitress showed the same indifference. The guy who had ordered the chitlins held his nose. The meat loaf was good, but not good enough to warrant the price. Everybody but one girl tried a bite of the chitlins. Junuh didn't tell them that back home people would douse their chitlins with hot sauce and vinegar, would eat them with corn bread instead of a biscuit. He did not tell them there was no such a thing as "black time," that his mother would have chewed out the waitress. He didn't want to spoil his friends' illusions. Besides, this black family had a good thing going. Soul food for spoiled white people. Let them wait, charge them double, and they'd still think they had been through a cultural experience. Junuh never went back to Claydon's.

It was during his residency that the eye of a hurricane hung offshore like a Cyclops. The weatherman said few before had been like this. Junuh called his mama and she said, "You'd have to come down here and drag him away, and if he ain't coming you'd have to drag me, too. No, Son, we weathered many a storm, and this be the same. You stay up there. We be fine down here."

Junuh had the choice between a cocktail party at the hospital administrator's house, which many of his senior colleagues would attend, or driving down home to force his aging parents to come inland from the storm. He decided to attend the party. His mother was right; he remembered other hurricanes washing past the house without serious consequences.

But when Hugo came ashore, it brought a surge that washed clean the yard where Junuh had played, took the house and his parents afloat, then swallowed them. When, finally, enough of the road had been cleared that Junuh could get in, he found only clean sand and an aluminum canoe cradled high in the tree boughs.

Junuh watched the flames turn. I should have gone down there and taken them away, even if I had to drag them. They sent me away to learn, and I knew that storm wasn't normal. I had learned that much. Sent me to learn what I'm not. Not a Gullah-speaking crab-potting nigger. Not a white man. Not even something between. A man who speaks numbers, writes words only he can understand. Don't let anyone else read it or they might say you are wrong. Write in your own words, be unto yourself. I can't walk on water, or heal the blind, and I'm not debating whether a man once could. I was educated not to be a fool, but here I am acting like one, out in the muck and grime with a dead man's ashes and two idiots less like me than the rain is.

Junuh had pulled the respirator. Nate's eyes had gotten softer then, as if the air he sipped was richer than that which had been pumped into him. He and Reese and Ruth were there when Nate flat-lined. No resuscitation. He'd written those words himself. Nate had flat-lined and been that way for nearly a minute when he suddenly sat straight up, beckoned at the window, smiled, and spoke these words:

"Inside the circle I'll return to you, and there you'll realize that you are where you started for."

Nate fell back, his breath fading from him, and the color drained from his feet up.

You are where you started for? Doesn't

make much sense. Narcotics talk. What? You never get away from where you start? Or, you were already there to begin with? A dying man telling me I left everything and nothing to sit here and slap mosquitoes. Mama wouldn't be too proud of me now.

Why does God have to send every man off into the wilderness to see the light, Reese wondered. I already believe, Lord. I don't need to see the burning bush.

He kept his eyes steady on the flames.

I've already seen the bush.

Absentmindedly, Reese broke a small stick into pieces, throwing them one by one into the fire. The center glowed blue where most of the heat was concentrated. Clean smoke, woodsy and fragrant, the vapor of natural life. So different from the smell of diesel fuel that belched from the exhaust of the Abrams tank in which Reese had been a radio communicator. He hadn't counted on the Gulf War starting when he joined the army.

His tank already had three kills, two Iraqi tanks that never had a chance, the other an artillery gun blasted into oblivion. All the kills had been from more than a mile away, warfare much like the Nintendo games he'd played as a boy, illuminated night screens, radar, the crackle of the radio in his earphones. When they fired the 120 millimeter, Reese felt the kick in his lower back. It vi-

brated through his bones, but most of the recoil was absorbed in the heavy armor plating of the tank. The hum and whine of machinery, commands and dialogue replaced by electrical impulses communicated through Reese's headphones. He was listening to a propaganda station when the alarm sounded. They were in the radar sights of an enemy tank. The crew had just jerked into motion when the shell hit with a jolt and a sharp crack. Lights flashed. Acrid smoke, glare of fire, a curious smell like meat frying. Only seconds had passed when Reese realized he was lying on the floor, his helmet off.

By instinct, he pulled the emergency hatch release and scrambled toward the stars in the late night sky. He dived face-first into sand, slapping at his smoldering trouser leg. He heard shouting as another tank from his squadron arrived. Arms lifted him by his shoulders and dragged him away.

Reese learned later that the shell had been friendly fire. Why he alone had escaped, he knew not, but the odds had been incredible. The other three crew members succumbed to fire and smoke.

The newest piece to the fire smoked first, then began to burn where the wood was most frazzled, yellow flames barely hot enough to singe. Ruth shrieked and pointed to the sky. "A shooting star!"

All eyes followed her arm, but the sky fire was gone.

"Must have been a big one to leave a

trail like that," Junuh said.

"This is one time I'm revealing my wish. I wish that we're all safely off this lake tomorrow."

"You better be praying, rather than wishing."

"I swear, Reese," said Ruth. "You could make a puppy weep. Don't you have the slightest bit of romance in you? Don't you believe in good-luck signs?"

Clearing his throat, Reese spat into the flames. "I just don't wish on them."

"Junuh, do you wish on falling stars?"

"I bet I haven't seen a falling star in ten years. When I was a kid, I used to wish on them."

"Wishing is the same as praying, Reese," Ruth said.

"It's not if you don't use the Lord's name with your wish. The Lord grants wishes."

"The Lord is in everything, Reese. If I say tree, I'm saying God. If I say rock, I'm saying God."

"It's not that easy, Ruth. You have to give up something to gain God. That tree can't forgive me of my sins."

"That tree doesn't blame you for your sins. Sins are in the mind of the beholder. They're not universal."

Reese spat again. "The sin of killing is not universal?"

Ruth laughed. "You just slapped and killed a mosquito."

"Yeah, a bug."

"It has life. I don't kill mosquitoes. I

brush them away."

"Well, good for you. You leave more for me and Junuh to combat."

"I don't kill anything without a reason."

"Hoo-ray. You're a regular Mother Teresa."

Reese sat silent for a moment before continuing in a more solemn tone. "There's a price for learning, Ruth. An old, old woman stands by the gates of heaven. Before she lets a person in, she eats the scars from their bodies so they enter heaven flawless."

He paused as Ruth's face tightened.

"If they don't have any scars, she eats their eyes. Anybody who didn't accumulate scars during life didn't really live."

"That's pretty deep, Reese," Ruth said. "I didn't know you had that in you."

"I'll enter heaven through Christ's shed blood, and I'll have my eyes, too. I don't just wish through life."

"Good! See, that hurricane was for a reason, Reese. Nate bringing us here was for a reason. A good reason. More scars. You just need to let go of your anger. Whatever it is, it's eating you alive."

Reese chuckled, but not with mirth. "Ruth, I know you mean well. But to me, you're like a fawn, or a little bird just hatched. You don't think shit stinks, 'cause you ain't never stepped in it."

A Purple Heart followed by a bad conduct discharge. A job for money to buy vodka, cheap vodka so Reese could sometimes afford drugs.

A ratty motel room that smelled of mildew. A woman kept knocking at the door. Reese already had tried three veins, but all had collapsed. The liquid heroin in the needle offered eight hours of sleep and relief. He'd lay watching Oprah if he wasn't sleeping and relish how good it felt not to feel. Reese found a vein, tied it off and thumped the skin, then inserted the needle and felt that rose bloom in his forehead. Feeling good and airy, he lay in a semi-stupor for half an hour when the knocking started again. A whore in a tight, short dress. Reese laid the needle down and went to tell her to go. When he opened the door he saw the same flash of flame that had been inside the tank, but the fire was cool and felt like mist on his skin. A man in a gray suit stood smiling in the center of the flames. Reese backed away. The whole room was full of light, and instead of mildew, he smelled flowers.

"Who are you?" Reese asked.

"You," the man answered.

Reese stared at the man, and it was himself, clean, hair combed, wearing a suit. "Why didn't we die in that tank with everyone else?"

"We had work to do."

"What work?"

"Comforting a person. We have to keep him comfortable until he knows where to go."

"What person?"

"You don't know him yet, but you will. There are many things you don't know yet."

Reese wasn't afraid. He'd hallucinated before. His well-dressed twin walked to the bedstand and opened the drawer. From it, he took the Gideon Bible. "Sit here on the bed beside me, Reese. I want to read to you."

"Why didn't we die in that tank? Everybody else did. Brown died. I didn't get a scratch."

"Brown didn't die. He just crossed over. Sit here and let me read to you."

Sunlight poured through the window as Reese cracked one eye open. The morning news was on TV. The Bible was still spread open on his chest. He thought of his visitor the previous night and wondered if he had been hallucinating or dreaming. His fifth of vodka was still half-full. Reese reached for it, then paused. He lifted the book from his chest and tried to focus on the words.

Reese snapped a branch and looked from the flames to Ruth. Seemed like such a long and unnecessary road to get to a campfire on a spit of land above a flood with a young man's ashes.

"You don't know what shit I've stepped in." Ruth was fighting to keep from showing her anger. "You have no idea of the realities of my life. Neither does Junuh."

"Junuh, you've been mighty quiet."

"I've argued enough in this life. I'd as soon be quiet."

"I love both of you," Ruth said.

Silence. The crackle of the fire and the hum of insects. Neither of the men responded. Ruth turned her back against the flames.

Now again into the wilderness and a man who seemed to come out of the shadows to speak insanity. In the silent recesses of his mind, Reese heard that alarm again — something incoming and volatile enough to burn him up.

Throughout the night, the fire burned slowly, the flame drying the green wood inch-by-inch and devouring it. The three humans twisted and turned, huddled in layers of sleep, swatting mosquitoes from inside fragments of dreams, chafed, chilly, miserable, hungry in that spent, hollow, exhausted level between existence and fantasy. The moon dropped toward the western horizon. Venus began to rise in the east. The sun was still an hour buried when the first bird blew one note and started the chain reaction that became dawn.

Reese was dreaming of the war. Sand was in his ears and down his collar. He was standing beside the fifty-cal gunner, and Iraqi soldiers were crying and shouting as they came from a bunker with arms lifted. Reese wished the men would shut up, or that the gunner would spray them with a burst and make them shut up. In the night sky came a flare, bright and silver. Or was that Venus? The screaming continued, and the desert sand suddenly became cold and wet.

Ruth knew she wasn't dreaming. A large snake lay across her leg, and beyond

the snake was another, and dozens more beyond that. No, this wasn't a bad dream. She
was beside a smoldering fire, still damp and
chilled from a hurricane, and the ground was
covered with snakes. I have descended into
hell, she thought. I died during the night. All
along, Reese was right, and now my sins have
caught me, and I am in the bowels of hell.

Ruth screamed from the bottom of her
lungs, an anguish and hopelessness that was
eternal.

"Sit still," Reese hissed. He clasped his
hand over Ruth's mouth. "Sit very still and
they won't bite you."

Above his hand, her eyes were huge,
brown and terrified. Her scream had awakened Junah. "Lay still, Doc. There's snakes
all around us. Move slowly if you have to
move at all."

Junuh's eyes jerked wide open. "What
did you say?"

"We're in the company of snakes. I
think they were seeking dry land. If you want
to sit up, do it slowly."

Very slowly and carefully, Junuh sat
up. Except for the snake that had awakened
Ruth, the reptiles had stopped about a yard
from the three humans and the heat of the
coals. More than a hundred reptiles in many
patterns and colors were coiled or crawled
in the small allotment of un-flooded ground.
"If I take my hand from your mouth, are you
going to scream?" Reese asked. Ruth shook
her head.

"Snakes can't hear," Junuh said.
"They're sensitive to heat and vibrations."

"What kind are they?" Reese asked.

"Looks like all types. I'm not a snake expert."

"What are we going to do?" Ruth asked. "God, I hope I wake up and I'm only dreaming."

"This ain't no dream," Reese said.

Time moved insufferably slowly, while the three sat in silence, not daring to move, awaiting daybreak. As light began to reveal itself, some of the snakes slithered into the bushes. Most, however, stayed in tight coils, occasionally flicking their tongues into the chill air.

"When the sun comes up, maybe they'll all leave," Junuh said.

"We get off this island, we won't have to worry about snakes," Reese said. "I bet every snake on the lake is here."

"I wish right now I'd studied toxicology instead of oncology," Junuh said. "I don't know a thing about treating snakebite."

"Believe me," Ruth said. "If one of those snakes bites me, the venom won't be a problem. I'll die from a heart attack."

When Son's skiff appeared, he poled the boat well into the trees because of the high water. He wore rubber boots that came nearly to his knees, and he slowly scanned the scene, his eyes taking in the snakes. He reached into the boat for his staff, then waded into the mass, sometimes bending, picking up a snake with one hand and tossing it aside, but more often carefully moving them with the pole toward the edge of the woods, the snakes flowing away like streams of water.

"We're seeing a miracle," Ruth said.

"We're seeing a nut," Reese replied.

"As long as he gets rid of these snakes, I don't care what he is," Junuh said.

After picking up a particularly bright snake with red and black stripes, Son held the serpent against the sky, seeming to admire the dance of light on its glittering scales. Carefully, he laid it in the edge of the forest. "Rainbow snake," he announced. "Harmless."

Son used his staff to move the next snake, thick-bodied, greenish-black, with bands across its back. It struck at the pole, mouth gaping and as white as a cloud inside. He carried the snake to the water's edge, where it sank and disappeared. "Cottonmouth," he stated. "*Agkistrodon piscivorus.* That snake will bite you!" He laughed. "Won't bite Son. Not if he sees it coming."

Junuh, Reese and Ruth watched in silent amazement, as Son cleared the camp. Drops of blood appeared on his hands and arms where some of the snakes had bitten him.

"That's amazing," Ruth said when he had finished. "My God, you're bitten!"

"*Mark* 16: 'They shall take up serpents, and if they drink any deadly thing, it shall not hurt them.'"

"Let me look at the bites," Junuh said. "I'm a physician."

"Physician. A person skilled in the art of healing. I need to be sick before I need healing."

"You were bitten by snakes."

"Pit vipers have elliptical pupils. Except for the coral snake, all snakes in America with round pupils are non-poisonous."

"You looked the snakes in the eye?" Reese asked.

"I'm looking you in the eye. You have round pupils."

Son stepped forward, then reached and took Reese's cross in his fingers. He turned the cross, the gold sparkling in the bright sunlight.

"Who are you?" Reese asked.

"Son."

"Son who?"

"Son of man."

Reese stepped backward, causing Son to release the cross. "That's blasphemy!"

"Blasphemy. The act of insulting or showing contempt or lack of reverence for God." Son reached again for the cross, but Reese pushed his hand away.

"That's blasphemy, and you're one crazy son of a gun."

"Cool it," Junuh said. "He got rid of the snakes."

"Where do you live?" Ruth asked.

Son turned to his left and pointed. "Paradise."

"Who do you live with at paradise?"

"Son."

"Yourself? Do you have a family?"

"Family. A group of people united by certain convictions or a common affiliation."

"A mother or father?" Reese exploded. "Sisters or brothers? Not some blame dictionary definition!"

"I am Son of man."

"Jesus fucking Christ," Junuh said.

"Don't say that," Reese admonished.

The song of birds and the whisper of the wind were interrupted by the cry of another animal, a high bleating noise of distress. Junuh held his hand up for silence. The noise came again from behind the camp where the woods were thick. Son lifted his chin and sniffed the air. He began walking, beckoning with his hand.

"Don't follow him," Reese said. "No telling what's out there."

The noise came again, a definite wail of pain and despair. At the edge of the forest, Son stopped and beckoned again.

"It's some sort of animal," Junuh said. "Sounds hurt."

Ruth began walking toward Son. "Come on. Show some balls. Some animal is hurt out there."

The fawn was mired in the swamp, struggling to hold its head above water. It was less than a year old, with large, scared brown eyes, its back still dappled with spots. It struggled at the sight of humans, bleated again, its tongue unusually pink against the dark muck that coated its muzzle. A couple of buzzards watched from the branches of a torn tree, as if awaiting the young animal's sentence. Ruth picked up a stick and flung it toward the large birds. Her aim was off, but the act was enough to rush the vultures into flight.

"We've got to get the poor thing out,"

she said.

Son stepped into the pool and sank immediately to the top of his boots, brown water flooding over the lips of rubber. A long snake crawled away into a thick bramble of wild blueberry bushes. For a moment, Ruth thought she might cry at the sight of the trapped deer. She thought of herself, of the muck and mire she had sunk into during the past three years, up to her neck and in danger of drowning, the beauty of simply loving someone dirtied by people with dark notions. She stepped into the pool and immediately was knee deep. She struggled until she was beside the animal, opposite Son.

"Come on, help," she called to Junuh and Reese.

By locking fingers with Son, Ruth was able to cradle the fawn's belly between them. Both grumbling, Reese and Junuh entered the pool. Junuh pushed against the deer's hind quarters, while Reese wrapped one arm around its neck.

"Don't break its neck, Reese," Ruth warned.

"I ain't going to break his neck!"

"On three. One... two... three."

The deer bleated and panted, its tongue lolling to one side. It struggled as the humans lifted, pulled and pushed. Water and mud flew, and frantic splashing announced that the creature's legs were free.

Back on land, the fawn tried to stand, but couldn't. Son stooped, picked it up and carried it to the campsite. Carefully, he laid it on the ground, then pointed at the goblet beside the cooking pot.

"Should I heat some water?" Ruth asked.

Son reached for the goblet, then kneeled beside the young deer. What he did next was clean and quick, finished before anyone realized what was happening. Putting down the goblet, he took a large folding knife from his pocket, and, with a flick of his thumb, opened the blade. With his free hand, he gripped the fawn's muzzle, pulled its head back until the neck was exposed, and sliced deeply into the flesh. The fawn began to bleat, the cry cut off suddenly as the wind pipe was severed. Blood spurted, and Son kept cutting until the animal's neck doubled back on it-self. He jammed the end of the blade into the earth, picked up the goblet and held it under the gush of blood.

Ruth screamed and slapped her hand over her eyes. Even Junuh and Reese recoiled.

"My God!" Junuh cried. "Why did you do that?"

The goblet was full of blood when Son lifted the cup toward the sky. He stared at fingers of bright red blood that ran down the sides of the vessel. "'And Moses said to them, it is the bread of which the Lord has given you to eat.'"

Ruth was still screaming.

"My God, man!" Reese shouted. "You want us to drink blood?" He slapped the cup from Son's hand. The blood was flung in a half arc that colored Junuh's trouser leg. Reese curled both fists. "Get out of here! You're evil. 'Get thee behind me, Satan!'"

Ruth had stopped screaming, but still whimpered. Son put his hands to his ears, his eyes shut tightly for a moment. He stood, walked quickly to his boat, and quickly slipped out of sight behind the trees.

"What do you think now?" Reese said. "I told you the man was crazy. Probably dangerous, too. He could have cut one of us as easily as that deer."

Ruth had composed herself. She kneeled and closed the open eye of the dead fawn. A pool of blood was gathering around its slit neck. "I'm sorry," she said softly. "I lost it for a moment."

"You didn't overreact," Reese said. "The lunatic slaughtered that deer right in front of us."

"He was offering us food," Ruth said. "Blood is protein. One of the primal foods."

"I ain't drinking blood," Reese said.

"You will if you get hungry enough," Junuh said. "We all will. If we don't get off of this lake, we'll turn on each other. That's the way of nature."

"We're human beings," Reese said. "Not animals. We're made in the likeness of God."

"You really think so?" Junuh replied. "Not from what I've seen of this world."

Son had been gone only a few minutes when Junuh turned on the radio. The news had just begun.

"Hurricane Dena continues to defy weather forecasters as she sits off the Virginia/North Carolina coastline, with sustained winds of one hundred and twenty miles per hour. Forecasters say the storm may increase in intensity and could turn back eastward and retrace her path across North Carolina."

Junuh turned the radio off. "God almighty! We've got to get off this lake today. That hurricane comes back through, we won't stand a chance."

"Well," Reese said, "let's get going."

"Son might have taken us in his boat if you hadn't scared him away," Ruth complained.

"Your screaming didn't help," Reese replied.

The three shared the boiled water that was left in the pot. Reese put the deer jerky and the can of Vienna sausage in his pack. He scanned the shoreline, the water over the banks and well into the forest.

"Walking out is going to be hell. Briers and mud, snakes. We'll be lucky to get to the truck before dark."

"What if we swim along the shore?" Junuh asked. "Might be easier than bushwacking."

Reese was silent for a moment. "I can't swim very well."

"You were in the Army, and you can't swim?"

"I was in armor. Wasn't any need to swim."

"I can only dog paddle," Ruth said. "I can walk faster."

Junuh shook his head slowly. "Let's get

going."

"What about Nate's ashes?" Ruth asked.

"Let's scatter them right here."

"He wanted more than that. He knew something."

"You carry them, then," Reese said. "I've got a bellyful of Nate's desires."

In an hour, the group had gone only about a hundred yards. Cat brier vines and devil's toothpick thorns ripped at their clothes and skin; the mud was often to their knees. Snakes frequently dropped from bushes and slithered away. Curses and prayers erupted. Ruth fell backward, the murky water encircling her waist. She held the urn above the water to protect it.

"I'm exhausted. I don't have the strength to move."

"We're never going to be able to walk out," Junuh said.

"We've got to try harder," Reese prodded. "Maybe the undergrowth will thin out." He helped Ruth to her feet. "That hurricane comes back through here, we're goners."

Reese led the way through another hour of struggle, hacking at reeds and vines with a hunting knife. He didn't see the hornet nest until he had knocked it from a branch. He heard the angry rattle, then felt a stab of fire on his neck as the first one hit him. In only seconds, all three were shouting, slapping, wheeling backward toward their camp. Junuh broke through the brush and dived into the lake. Reese and Ruth followed, not caring how deep the water was.

Among them, they had a couple dozen

stings. Reese had taken the worst of the assault, eleven welts rising on his forearms and face. He stood in waist-deep water, his arms outstretched. He wished for a cigarette, any drug that might ease the acid that circulated in his blood. But his cigarettes were gone, the last one smoked to the filter an hour earlier.

"I'm going back," Ruth announced. "This is foolishness. At least we have dry ground and a fire at the campsite."

"And a million snakes," Reese added. "And a lunatic with a big knife."

"We need to build a big fire," Ruth said. "Lots of smoke. People know we're here. I'm supposed to be back on shift tomorrow night. People will come looking."

"I think she's right," Junuh said. "We'll never walk out of here. I don't think Son is dangerous. Maybe he'll agree to take us out in his boat."

"I think y'all are forgetting that a major hurricane is sitting off the coast. If it comes back this way, and we're on this lake, we'll drown this time."

"Why are you so afraid of dying, Reverend?" Junuh asked. "You seem so sure of heaven, yet you're awfully afraid of going there."

"I'm not afraid of dying," Reese said, spitting the words. "But life is sacred. Giving up is the same as suicide." He took a handful of mud and spread it over the welts on his arms. "You two go on back. Build a fire. Build a big one. Me, I'm going to get out of here."

The trio struggled onward for another hour, at times waist-deep, until pulling each foot free to take another step was a major effort. Often they had to skirt trees that had fallen during the storm, their path a zigzag that robbed them of energy. The sun read mid-afternoon when Reese lost his balance and staggered backward. He closed his eyes for several seconds, taking deep breaths.

"Okay, we've maybe gone a mile since we left the camp. Following the curve of the lake, we're probably still four miles to the truck. We can't make it this way. I've prayed the last hour, and this swamp doesn't end."

"I've prayed too, Reese," said Ruth. "We're just not meant to walk out of here."

"Well, what do we do? Stay here and die?"

"We go back to the camp, Reese. Build a big fire and rest. People will start looking for us soon."

"I agree," Junuh said. "We can't walk out."

"Maybe I can build a raft," Reese said. "A couple of logs lashed together and I could float right across this lake. It's not far straight across."

Reese noticed the leech on the back of his hand then, a black, tear-shaped glob about an inch long. When he pulled it from his skin, a pinpoint of blood appeared. "Leeches. We're probably covered with them. I don't want to even look under my clothes."

"Then don't," Ruth answered. "Let's turn around, Reese. We tried. No one can say we didn't try."

"If I just had the faith." Reese said despondently. "The *Bible* says it. If I had faith the size of a mustard seed, God would make a bridge right across the water."

"It's not your fault, Reese. Let's just go back. We'll build a big fire. We'll rest, and help will come."

Chapter 6

The trip back was only slightly easier. Enough of their trail was visible that they stayed single file and pushed forward, each alone with his or her thoughts. Only occasionally were words exchanged. Beneath his clothing, Reese was aware of itches, but he tried to force his mind away from ticks and leeches slowly draining him of blood. Instead, he thought of the raft he might build, something he could lie on and paddle across the water. Maybe the storm would start moving out to sea, and getting off the lake quickly would not be so necessary. Reese wondered what Ruth and Junuh were thinking. Did they itch? Did they blame him for not leading them out of the swamp?

The waistband of her jeans and the bra strap on her back were the places bothering Ruth. She wanted to push her hand down into her pants, but the thought of slimy, black leeches so disgusted her that she took deep breaths and concentrated on each step, thought of the fire they would build and the warmth it would bring. She was so tired that memories and dreams muddled.

She was sleeping when she felt Bob's hand on her shoulder. She opened her eyes, blinked them clear of sleep, and saw her boyfriend standing beside the bed. She pulled herself up until she rested against the headboard. Through the window, the sun was still below the horizon, the eastern sky an umbrella of pale dawn.

"You're already dressed. Where are you going so early?"

Bob sat on the edge of the bed and took Ruth's hand, his face weary and sad.

"You look like you didn't sleep all night," she said.

"I didn't. I was thinking about us."

Ruth squeezed his hand. "It was just a little argument. We'll work these things out."

"No, we won't, Ruth. It's the same argument over and over, and I'm so sick of it, I could die. I don't know you anymore. You place crystals on altars, and all these new friends of yours chant and pray to trees. You're not the woman I fell in love with."

Ruth felt the blood rise in her cheeks. "I let you have your friends, Bob. Your golf weekends. Your fishing trips."

"But we don't have any common friends anymore. You've rejected all of our old friends. You won't even eat the fish I catch."

"Well, you won't give my new friends a chance. You're so critical."

"They pray to trees! They rub crystals

on each other."

"They don't pray to trees, Bob. It's the spirit in the trees. Crystals have powers. If you'd just try them. Open up a little bit."

"Open what? Get naked and pass a crystal around a campfire? I wasn't raised that way."

"You're not feeding the spirit in yourself."

"You're not feeding me! Brown rice and tofu? The spirit in me would starve on that stuff."

"Fried chicken and gravy and biscuits and..."

Bob pulled his hand back and stood, interrupting her. "See, we can't talk. We can't sit down and communicate. We can't make love without incense and candles burning."

"We could communicate if you'd just listen to me. Really hear me!"

Bob held up his hand. "Here we are arguing again. The sun isn't up, and we're arguing. I can't take this any longer, Ruth. I'm moving out for a while. You need to decide what you really want in life. I don't think it's me anymore."

Ruth felt her stomach twist. "Don't go, Bob. We'll get counseling."

"We've been to every counselor in town! You don't think you can fart without someone advising you if the moon is right or not. We can't carry on a conversation without you calling someone to interpret my words."

"You're always attacking me. You belittle everything I say."

Bob snorted. He laughed without the slightest mirth, bent and kissed Ruth's forehead, then walked to the door. "I love you, Ruth, but I can't keep living like this. I'll be in touch."

Ruth heard the rustle of bags from the living room, then the front door opening and closing. She wanted to cry, wished that she could cry, but the tears weren't there. Did she love him? Had she truly ever loved him?

Ruth's attraction to women had always been there, the shape of their bodies, their fragrance, gracefulness, attention to detail. At thirteen, she and one of her friends had practiced French kissing with each other, their reasoning that the experience would be good when that first date with a boy finally came along. Although something inside Ruth whispered that what she was doing was wrong, the warmth of another set of lips against hers felt right. Her aunt and uncle never touched her, offered none of the hugs and kisses she had been so used to receiving from her parents, and the pulse and heat she felt from Debbie was like a balm, an elixir, a potion that left her dizzy.

Then one day Debbie put her hand on Ruth's breast, and she didn't stop her. Her nipple hardened immediately and tingled. Debbie pulled her shirt up and slipped her hand beneath her bra. Ruth did the same to her friend. And if the sound of steps on the stairs hadn't announced the arrival of one of her cousins...well, Ruth always wondered what might have happened.

That night Ruth prayed to Mother Mary and asked forgiveness. She and Debbie stopped kissing and began to see less of each other. Ruth's Catholic training was clear about sex — or the lack of it without the sanctity of marriage — and the electric charge she had felt when Debbie squeezed her nipple was terrifying. Yet for all her guilt, she couldn't truly believe that the simple act of touching another person was wrong. Yet the world made that fact all too clear.

But after a failed marriage and several boyfriends, Ruth felt burned, deceived, rejected by men. She met Brenda at a spa and allowed intuition to guide her. When Brenda asked her to dinner, she didn't hesitate, although she had no doubts about her intentions.

After Brenda came Carla, and Ruth discovered that men and women argued about the same things that eventually ended relationships. She ventured deeper into her own spirituality — treasuring nature, sunsets and nighttime skies. Alone, she often wept in the darkness, and whenever her body needed fulfillment, mind and hand became her lover.

Ruth focused her memories to keep from thinking about what might be under her clothes. She itched in a dozen places, and though she knew leeches were as worthy of life as songbirds, the thought of them fat with her blood made her want to rip off her clothes and rake at the places where she itched. Will

we ever get out of this swamp? she asked herself. Will we ever get back to camp? Please
God.

      Junuh had encountered leeches in the
creeks and swamps where he grew up. He
considered them to be in the same category
as wasps and hornets, creatures capable of
causing great misery, always to be avoided.
He had snatched several from his trousers
and knew that many must be under his
clothes. The thought repulsed him, but he
remembered that the bite of a leech was not
considered dangerous. He knew that in medical history, and even now, leeches were used
for medical purposes, and that "leech" actually once was a name for physicians. If leeches
actually purified the blood, as many once
believed, he was certain that his probably was
free of any taint by now. It wasn't the first
time he'd felt preyed upon.

      *Following his residency and accep-
tance of a staff position at Memorial Hospital, Junuh felt pulled in all directions. Every
social and business organization in Chapel
Hill wanted him. The Jaycees hounded him
to join and increase their sparse minority rep-
resentation. So did the Elks and Lions. Big
Brother in Durham had called him half a
dozen times.*
      *"Mr. Parrott, you're the very kind of
man we're looking for. You're successful, ar-
ticulate, educated — the very example we're*

seeking for young men from the projects."

"I appreciate the interest. I certainly do. But you don't understand how little free time I have. Most nights I don't leave the hospital until eleven."

"Couldn't you work with one boy? We're only asking for a couple of hours a week. These kids need to see that selling drugs is not a way out of poverty."

"Look, sir, I'd like to, but I never know when I'll be called back to the hospital. There have to be other men who don't have my schedule."

"We need someone these kids can identify with and look up to."

In time, the organizations quit calling.

Donna worked at Nationwide Insurance, where Junuh had policies on his house and car. She had a nice voice and was witty, very helpful whenever he called. Junuh created reasons to call her. Would the new addition to his house need extra coverage? Was a Jeep Wrangler more expensive to insure than a car? Eventually, they talked about things other than business, and Donna noted they had the same astrology sign. She said she admired doctors, that her elderly mother was spry due to the excellent medical treatment she had received following her broken hip. When Junuh finally got up the nerve to ask her out for a drink, she hadn't hesitated in saying yes.

They agreed to meet at Bud and Eb's Restaurant on a Friday afternoon. She said she would be in a red jacket. Junuh told her to look for a guy in Dockers and a green polo shirt. His jacket would be over his shoulder. When Donna came through the door, Junuh recognized her immediately and met her extending his hand. He hadn't asked her to describe herself, but was pleased at the lithe woman with blue eyes that she turned out to be. She smiled broadly, but Junuh noticed that her up-turned mouth didn't seem natural. It looked almost painted on. During their first drink, Donna jiggled her foot constantly, checking the door often, folding her napkin carefully into a tight square.

"Am I different from what you expected?" Junuh finally asked.

"Oh, no, not at all."

He had learned much about body language from his work.

"Really? You seem ill at ease."

Donna laughed. "Okay, I'll be brutally honest, but sincerely, this doesn't matter at all. I was raised in California."

"Okay, be brutally honest."

"I thought you were white. The way you speak, I thought maybe you were from Connecticut. Had gone to an Ivy League school."

Junuh nodded slowly. "I guess all the schooling and going back home so infrequently took away my accent. Does it bother you, me being black? Be honest."

"I am. Really, no it doesn't bother me. I was just surprised. I've dated black men. It's just your voice." She laughed again. "You sound like you went to Harvard."

They went to a movie at the Chelsea, a small theatre that showed mostly foreign films and served wine in the lobby, but they never went out again.

Junuh spied another leech on his arm and thumped it away with his middle finger. He knew there had to be dozens under his clothes.

Reese was first to spot the smoke from their campfire. Another quarter mile at most. They just had to keep putting one leg in front of the other until they got there. Then they could strip off their clothes and roll like dogs on the earth, popping engorged leeches, right back at the spot where they had started this dismal day, no closer to rescue despite all the misery and frustration they had suffered.

The fawn Son killed that morning had been gutted, skinned and skewered by two long green poles. The carcass was suspended about three feet above a fire that obviously had been tended throughout the day. Dripping fat and juice hissed against the embers.

The three people stood staring at the ready meal.

"Well, he means for us not to go hungry," Ruth said. "He seemed to know we'd be back. I think my vegetarianism is going on hold for tonight."

"I felt like we were being watched," Reese said.

"I can't say I'm sorry he went ahead

and made supper," Junuh put in. "Another hour and that meat will be right."

Staring at the smoking fawn was a good excuse not to have to look under their clothes, but that concern couldn't be put aside. Ruth sat in the chair and began to roll up one pants leg. The first leech she saw was swollen to the size of her thumb. She grasped it with her fingers and yanked. It separated from her, but stung as it came free, leaving a mark on her skin. She slung it into the bushes, then leaned forward and retched. Only a string of saliva hung from her lip.

"I can't do this," she moaned. "I'll faint. I know I'll faint."

Junuh kneeled and looked at the spot where the leech had been attached. "We can't just pull them off. Part of the leech's sucking apparatus is still in your skin. It'll get infected."

Ruth looked at him, her eyes shiny with tears. She gripped his arm. "Junuh, I don't like leeches. There are probably a hundred of them on me right now, and I'm going to freak out if I don't get them off me NOW." She tightened her grip. "Do you understand me?"

"I understand. Take a deep breath and let me think."

Reese pulled his shirt over his head, keeping his eyes closed. "How many are on me? I need to know, Junuh."

Ruth took a deep breath and buried her face into her knees. Reese was covered with leeches, his skin almost black with them, some engorged, others smaller, only recently adhered. They gleamed like globs of motor oil.

"How many are on me?" he asked again. "Just tell me, and I can cope with it."

"Maybe a couple hundred," Junuh answered. "What about fire? Maybe if we got a hot stick."

Ruth screamed then and began to fumble at the buttons on her shirt. When she wasn't nimble enough to open the first button after a couple of seconds, she ripped it off. Then holding the two sides of her shirt, she began yanking, screaming, her eyes like the yearling's when they were trying to pull it from the muck. Junuh grabbed her hands, but she kept screaming, and Reese came to help hold her. She cursed and clawed at them, even tried to bite them.

"Easy, Ruth, easy," Junuh whispered. "We'll get them off you. You've got to work with us."

The men pushed her to the ground and held her. Her skin was as covered as Reese's. Reese raked his fingers across them without effect. "Want me to yank them off, Doc?"

"We've got to find another way."

"Use this."

Both men were startled by the words. Son stood at the edge of the clearing, his hands filled with gray mushrooms.

Junuh's mouth dropped open. He hadn't heard Son's approach, hadn't seen his boat on the sandbar.

"What the hell do you have there?"

"Mother called it turtle back," Son said, raising his arms. "Good to ward off leeches, mosquitoes and chiggers. The Indians used them."

Ruth calmed on hearing Son's voice. Junuh lifted his hand and motioned Son forward. "How do you use them?"

Son moved quickly. He bent over Ruth and looked into her eyes. He divided the mushrooms between his hands and squeezed those in his right hand until drops of moisture ran between his fingers. The stench was vile.

"*Psalms* 139:8: 'If I ascend up into heaven, thou art there; and if I make my bed in hell, behold, thou art there.'"

"My bed is now in hell," Ruth whispered.

As Son rubbed the mass of mushrooms across Ruth's stomach, the leeches began falling away. Ruth sat up. Son washed her with the mushrooms, and the leeches fell from her back like black hail. She stood, unzipped her jeans, and pulled them to her feet. Her legs, too, were covered, but they fell from Son's hand as if he were shaving her with the sharpest of razors.

"It's a miracle," Ruth said.

"Miracle," Son repeated, then shook his head. "An extraordinary event manifesting divine intervention in human affairs. All of life is a miracle, Ruth."

"And the miracles come from God," Reese said. "Not from a man with a fistful of mushrooms."

Junuh was already unbuttoning his shirt. "Let's not look a gift horse in the mouth right now."

Son used the mushrooms to free Junuh and Reese from the leeches as well, then gave mushrooms to each person so that they could turn away in privacy and expel the leeches beneath their underwear.

"How did you know we would need these mushrooms?" Ruth asked.

"The swamp is full of leeches," he said. As Ruth was pulling up her jeans, Son reached to touch a pink flower that was embroidered on the strap between her bra cups. Reese tried to push his arm away, but Ruth stopped him. "He means no harm, Reese."

Son traced the flower with his fingertip, then slowly dropped his arm.

"Come with me to paradise."

"Mister, we appreciate your help, but we're getting off this lake. There's only one paradise, and I don't think you're Saint Peter."

"Milton, *Paradise Lost*: 'To ask or search, I blame thee not, for heav'n is as the book before thee set, Wherein to read his wondrous works, and Learn His seasons, or hours or days, or months, or years.'"

"Look, maybe you know poetry, but that ain't the *Bible*. Maybe you know how to get rid of leeches, but I'll trust in the Lord to lead me to paradise."

"You can't speak for all of us," Ruth said. "Does he look dangerous? All he's ever done is try to help us!"

"He was touching your breast! About to, if I hadn't raised my hand."

"He was touching a flower! My God, Reese. Can't you see how blind you are?"

"I can see how naive you are. A turd doesn't stink in your world."

Son walked back to the edge of the clearing and returned with a headless chicken and a hefty watermelon. He placed both by the fire. From his belt, he pulled a large knife and jammed its tip several inches into the melon. Then he turned, went back to his boat and disappeared in silence.

"My God," Junuh said. "Take me home, country roads!"

He plucked the feathers from the fowl and gutted it, as he had many times in his youth.

"Mama would wring the chicken's neck," he said. "After it quit flopping, me and Cleo had to dip it in scalding water and pluck it. Made the feathers come off easier, that hot water. But the smell, Lord, the chicken would empty its bowels in the water. Ain't nothing worse than wet, shitty chicken feathers. We'd pluck the feathers and fuss over who was doing the most work, then carry it inside to Kareen, my older sister. She'd usually make us take it back out and clean it better. All she had to do was say, 'I'll tell Daddy,' and we were back cleaning that chicken right. Then Kareen would take out the liver and the gizzard, save the feet, and cut the rest of it into frying pieces. Didn't hardly nothing get thrown away. Those were good days. I'm starting to see that now."

Even Ruth tried to help with the cooking, despite her disdain for meat. Because they had little hot water, Junuh used an old trick for singeing off the smaller feathers.

"Whoever eats the most chicken will eat the most feathers," he warned with a smile.

The chicken, like the fawn, was skewered on a green stick and suspended above the flames.

Ruth searched the woods again before dark, salvaging a few pieces of cooking gear. She found a sleeping bag tangled in tree branches. It was torn but it would be more comfortable than the bare ground.

The watermelon was already half eaten when she returned. Junuh had devoured one slice down to the pale, green rind.

"Needed some salt," he said, grinning. "A little salt would have made it just right."

"Salt on watermelon?" Ruth wrinkled her brow. "I never heard of such a thing."

"Salt on watermelon. Pepper on cantaloupe. Wouldn't have it any other way."

"What did you do, take an elective on watermelons in pre-med?" Ruth asked.

Reese chuckled. Junuh cut his eye at him. "Go on. Say it, Reese."

"Naw. Naw. I ain't getting into that."

"Say it. I already know what you're chuckling about."

Reese laughed again, shaking his head. Then he laughed so hard for about fifteen seconds that he began coughing and gasping for air. He pointed at Junuh's rind, then broke out laughing again. Junuh began laughing, too.

"Will you please tell me what the joke is?" She grabbed Junuh's arm. The laughter was infectious, and she began giggling, too.

Reese stammered and stuttered, pointing at the rind. "The way you cleaned that slice of watermelon, if we'd had it on a string dangling out front, you'd have dragged us through that swamp today."

The two laughed so hard that they rolled to their sides against the ground.

Junuh beat the dirt with his fists. He started speaking and stopped twice before he could get the words out. "If you'd had a leg of fried chicken on that string, I'd have cleared a road right out to the truck."

The men laughed until tears rolled down their faces. Ruth found herself laughing as well, although she didn't know why.

"Lordy, Lordy," Junuh said when he could speak again. "I ain't laughed like that in so long."

"Me either," Reese said. "It's good to laugh. Sometimes I feel like I've forgotten how."

"Me too. Lord, Lord, me too."

"I still don't know why you were laughing," Ruth said.

"Ruth, I forget how Yankee you are," Junuh said. "You haven't — you ain't never heard the jokes about black people and watermelon? Or black people and fried chicken? About how we love it so much?"

"No!"

"Well, you better learn. A nigger cut you over his watermelon. And you ever raise any chickens, a nigger live nearby, you better lock the hen house door."

Reese laughed again, but covered his mouth with his hand in an attempt to stop.

"Ain't that right, Reese?"

"It's funny, but if I said what you just did, the Chapel Hill paper would be branding me a racist."

"And you probably would be if you said that, although I'm starting to think you're no more racist than anyone else. But it's true. My daddy on a Sunday afternoon with a fat, chilled Sugar Baby watermelon and his salt shaker. I can see him right now. And my brother Cleo. You want to see somebody that could put away some fried chicken. Mama used to cook one whole chicken just for him. He loved best the liver and the gizzard, cooked up with some onions."

Junuh's eyes got distant and shiny. "I've lost so much of myself — who I really am. Since I finished medical school, I wouldn't eat watermelon even if everybody else in the room did. Fried chicken, I'd only buy it from a drive-through at night. I was brain-washed. Nigger food, poor people's food. I quit eating the shad roe that I loved so much as a kid, but at a Chapel Hill party if there was caviar, I made sure some was on my plate."

"I'm sorry we made you feel ashamed," Ruth said.

"Who? White people? White people didn't make me feel ashamed. I knew why Reese was smiling 'cause it was on my mind, too. But, I did it to myself. Turned my back on who I was, on my heritage. My very language. Talked like a honky from Harvard. Thought I couldn't be a good doctor and a black man, too. Had to look and talk like Dr. Kildare. Had to lose my accent and change

my vocabulary. Ain't couldn't be a word, and
fried chicken a food."

Junuh threw his rind in the fire. "And
for what? To become a ghost? There ain't five
people in this world who would cry at my
funeral. I lost my tongue, my mama and
daddy, and I lost Nate. And in the past couple
of days, I've found out I've lost all respect
for myself. And I'm scared, Reese. I'm scared,
Ruth. I think I'm going to die right here on
this lake without a hint of who I am."

"You're not going to die," Reese said.
"I'm crossing that lake tomorrow. I think I
have a mustard seed in me. I think I have
that much faith."

Chapter 7

The rising sun found Reese and Junuh standing in knee-deep water, securing two cedar logs together with strips of tent fabric that Ruth had salvaged. During the night, they had burned off the ends of the logs so that both were about five feet long. They kept most of Reese's body out of the water. He figured that by lying with his knees at the end of the raft, he could kick with his legs and pull the water with his arms and be able to progress across the lake. A knapsack Ruth had put together contained a plastic bottle of water, some venison and a Ziploc bag containing a few of the mushrooms that were so effective against leeches.

The raft was not nearly as buoyant as Reese hoped, but he figured it should keep him from drowning. As he gazed across the lake, the white caps resembled a flight of birds against a clear sky. He thought of Peter from the *Bible* and of how he could walk on water when he trusted fully in Jesus, and of how the day before he had mired to his knees in the mud. A man's faith was supposed to allow him to move mountains, yet Reese had been unable to pull a fawn from the mud. And now he was being counted on to cross two miles of open water. He felt shame at his fear. If only God would anoint the shameful, Reese knew he could skip across that water.

Ruth held Reese's knapsack. "Be sure to drink water often. You could get dehydrated quickly in all this heat."

"I'm surrounded by water, Ruth."

"Not clean water. And you need to eat the meat. Think of it as gas."

"Then I better think of myself as a riding lawn mower cutting a path out of this hell hole."

The first quarter mile was deceptively easy. The water was smooth, the wind shielded by the trees along the shoreline. By marking the time it took to reach a selected tree, Reese estimated he was traveling at about a quarter of a mile an hour. He wasn't leaving much of a wake, but if he maintained his speed, he ought to make the landing by dark. He'd call 911, and the other two ought to be off the lake by midnight.

The raft was stable as long as Reese kept his weight distributed. He still could see the sandbar and a plume of smoke from the campfire. He still was within the cove, but the point of land that opened into broad lake drew closer and closer. His truck was about two miles straight across open water. By not following the undulating shoreline, he ought to be able to cross the lake before darkness. Motivation would fuel him more than meat and water. He was more than ready to be away from snakes, the crazy swamp man, and people who worshipped a different God, or no God at all.

Reese lifted his face from the log and peered at the sun, growing fierce as it rose higher. A turtle's head poked from the water, its black eyes trained on the log-joined man. It floated like an iceberg with only a small circle of shell exposed, the creature wondering at a man so out of place. Reese's neck and shoulder muscles ached from having his neck stretched to the side. Hurt like Hades. Reese could tell from a log on shore that he hadn't gained more than a few yards because of the wind. And almost as sure as the sun, the pain in his neck, and that turtle floating, God wasn't in the mood for making miracles today any more than he'd been for the past two thousand years.

Before the night Reese came face to face with himself in that cheap motel room, he eventually would have let the whore in when his high called for companionship. When the dope and alcohol were working good, he'd have answered her knock. But, when he started reading that Gideon *Bible, he went from word to word, sentence to sentence, and, over weeks, from* Genesis *to* Revelation, *absorbing each story and fitting it into a religion that was personal and unique.*

Reese was saved at a tent revival in a field adjacent to a Wal-Mart. When the call came from the minister for the sinners to come forward, Reese hesitated only a mo-

ment, then walked briskly down that aisle.
Paper funeral-parlor fans swished the heat
like hands waving to him. He was baptized
that night, along with about thirty other
people. He gave his word and every dollar in
his pocket to that preacher, and when he
walked from that tent, the stars in the sky
had a pattern he never had noticed before.

He became ordained through a corre-
spondence course. After much prayer, he
moved to Chapel Hill, where so many young
people at the university were tempted constantly by a town and a culture that Reese
thought stressed too much the impact of
youth and free thinking. He had a ready pul-
pit on the stone wall that was close to the
entrance of the student union and a hospital
with dozens of people standing daily on the
threshold of eternity. Because of the transient
student population, work was easy to find,
and as a butcher, Reese pretended he was a
man of Biblical days, slaughtering a lamb for
the Lord. Quickly, he became the best butcher
at Harris Teeter. He wore his thick, black hair
combed back like Elvis, and he found that
customers asked for him by name when they
needed meat cut to order. Sometimes he got
tips that he graciously accepted and used to
help finance his ministry. Occasionally, he
was offered other things.

"No ma'am, I can't, I'm married." He
held up his hand. "I just don't wear a ring at
work."

Reese reasoned he was married to
Christ, and a white lie meant in good intent
was harmless. The first couple of times he

had accepted a woman's proposal, he had found out quickly how wise he had been in coming here where the gospel was so needed.

The first date and she was kissing his neck, her flesh hot, perfume strong; she whispered in his ear. Reese had to stop quickly.

"I, I'm sorry. I don't even know you. And if I did...I mean I couldn't...I...I couldn't do that."

"You're gay, aren't you? I should have realized you're gay."

"Noooo. No. No. No. It's not that. Far from it. Let me talk to you. Let me tell you about the Lord...."

She didn't stay around to listen. Reese learned the white lie about being married was adequate for most women. And he wished his marriage wasn't a lie, that at night he lay in bed with a woman he loved, holding her to himself in refuge against the world. Then he might be able to sleep. Too many images became alive when Reese closed his eyes for deep sleep to come easily. The Devil was too alive in this world.

Reese first saw the raccoon as a spot on the water. He figured it was a turtle, but as the animal cut the water with a V-shaped wake, he realized it wasn't a reptile. The spot slowly got closer and closer until Reese could see a head and ears and finally the distinctive black mask.

Why in the heck would a 'coon swim way out here, Reese wondered. Got a whole forest to live in.

Reese didn't become alarmed until the animal was only about ten yards from the raft and closing. The raccoon panted for breath. No doubt it was coming for the logs, wasn't simply swimming across the lake.

"Get away from here!" Reese shouted. "Scat!" He paddled with one hand and turned to face the raccoon. "Get away from here."

The raccoon struggled to climb onto the raft, right at Reese's head. He flailed his arms and shouted, but the raccoon growled, and caught hold of a log, upsetting his precarious balance. The raft rolled over, pitching Reese and the animal under water. Reese clung to the logs and pulled himself to the surface; sputtering and coughing, he wiped the water from his eyes only to see the raccoon clawing back on board. Reese felt for the sheath knife on his belt. Twice more the movements of the nearly drowned creatures caused the raft to roll, the two fighting to climb back on top and breathe.

The raccoon didn't look right to Reese. Its eyes were dull and sticky with goop. It was thin. This time it climbed onto the logs with him, Reese shuffling backward, his heart pounding. The raccoon growled once, then leapt, sinking his fangs into Reese's right cheek. Reese thrust with his knife, the blade side turned upward as he had been taught in combat training. Twice he stabbed the raccoon; the animal bit deeply into Reese's flesh. The logs rolled again, and when Reese surfaced, the raccoon was swimming toward land, a plume of red blood trailing him.

The alligator struck like a battering ram, his head coming a couple of feet out of the water, the raccoon splay-legged within the alligator's jaws. When the reptile submerged, only swirls and fingers of blood marked where the death had occurred. Reese vomited lake water, then pulled himself back on top of the raft. He lay as still as possible, praying as the sun warmed his back. He balanced carefully so that his feet and hands were out of the water.

From where Ruth sat in the sand, Reese was only a spot she barely could see upon the water. She had spent most of the day between the fire and the sandbar where she observed Reese's painfully slow trek. She had sent prayers to every goddess, god, and prophet she could think of. Feeling a presence, Ruth turned to see Junuh standing behind her.

"He's almost out of sight now."

"Where?"

"That spot just out from the point. See his red shirt?"

"Oh, yeah. The wind is hitting him now. We'll see what kind of faith he has."

"You sound like you hope he fails."

Junuh sighed. "No. I just can't stand to hear what he'll say if he 'saves' us."

"A few minutes ago he seemed to be struggling. Maybe the raft turned over. I couldn't tell from here."

"The way this lake has been stirred up, I wouldn't want to be on this water. He's no coward. Actually, I'm starting to like him better."

"He was in the Gulf War," Ruth said. "I

wonder how that affected him."

"He's a strange man. He intimidates me, Ruth, and that bothers me. I shouldn't be intimidated by a man like him."

"What kind of a man is he?"

Junuh kicked the sand. "A redneck. Sort of a bully. I don't think he's a racist. Maybe that's what bothers me. He doesn't fit any definition. In Chapel Hill, everyone fits a certain category."

"Which one do you fit, Junuh?"

He chuckled. "These last couple of days have started me wondering. I probably would have said, 'liberal, black professional who has distanced himself from his roots.' I might be more truthful if I said 'follow-the-herd black professional who is ashamed of the very people and traditions that made him success-ful.'"

"You're being hard on yourself."

"I don't know, Ruth. There's a man out there floating on two tree trunks who I think would die for what he believes in if it came to that. I don't want to be like him, but I swear, I can't think of anything I'm passionate enough about to bet ten dollars on. I received all my schooling at UNC, and I can't even tell you the names of two starters on the basket-ball team."

Ruth covered her face with mock dis-may. "My God, Junuh. Now that is heresy in any religion!" She dropped her hands from her face and looked into Junuh's eyes. "You're being very hard on yourself, Doctor. I hap-pen to think you're a good man."

"What is a man, Ruth? There's a wide

134

range between the human being standing here on this sand and the human being out there floating on those logs."

"I think you just answered your question. I think you've come closer to learning what a human being is, Junuh. Reese is still pretty caught up in trying to be a man. You're successfully learning to blend the two."

Junuh stared at the lake thinking of what Ruth had just said. What does a woman know about being a man? he wondered. Blend the two? Yeah, right. Put all the colors together and what do you get? Black.

At the front door, Junuh took a deep breath and pressed the doorbell. The white woman who greeted him was dressed in designer sweater and slacks. She lived in a nice house in a manicured neighborhood, was a professional with one child, married to another professional. Inside the house were about fifty other people, their lives almost mirror copies of the woman who greeted him.

"Hello Junuh. I'm so happy you were able to come. Leaning, she kissed his cheek, one of her hands on his shoulder. "Congressman Rice got here just a few minutes ago." Taking his arm, she led him into the house. "What are you doing alone again? Handsome as you are, you ought to have a woman on each arm."

"Dating and doctoring don't mix too well."

She leaned slightly closer. "There's someone here I want you to meet. She hap-

pens to be a physician, too."

Classical music played softly. A table in the middle of the living room was laden with crackers and cheeses, dips, sliced vegetables and a whole, steamed salmon. Small groups of people chatted, sipping wine or mixed drinks. Junuh was led straight to the congressman and introduced.

"Well, it's a pleasure to meet you, Doctor. Certainly a pleasure." The man's handshake was too limp for Junuh. During small talk, the congressman managed to get in that he was a big supporter of the Black Student Union. The man's teeth were very white, every hair in place. Junuh slipped away when the congressman was in conversation with another man. Going to the table, he began filling a plate. At least the food was always good.

As usual, Junuh was the only black person at the party. As usual, the room was filled with white, professional liberals. There just weren't enough educated blacks in Chapel Hill to go around for all the parties during the holiday season. When Junuh did date a woman, she usually was white, not that he preferred white women, but he never ran into black women in Chapel Hill who weren't cleaning houses. And usually he didn't take the woman out again because he had his ways, and she had her ways, and they usually didn't mix very well. So, he went to the parties and sipped the wine and ate the brie, even though he knew he was the token black that all the concerned, conscientious whites could make a point of speaking to. Why did he go? Because he was lonely, and white women in red sweaters with sprigs of holly in their hair looked so different from people sick from chemotherapy. And Ivy-League educated men who talked of golf were always careful of what they said.

"You got to where you a big nigger now, ain't 'cha?" Kareen stood with her hand cocked on her ample hip. Junuh's eldest sister lived with her four children on the outskirts of Savannah, the house smelling strongly of hair dressing and bacon fat. A mongrel dog barked to be let in. "I slap you so hard your thick lips wrap around your nappy head!"

"I'm not criticizing you, Kareen. I just want your children to have the opportunity..."

"To what? Live up there with all them white people with their condescending minds. I standing there with you in that fancy sto' and the woman ask me where the butter is. She figure I black, I got to be sto' help."

"Shaqueena doesn't have to go to UNC, Kareen. I just want to help out. She can go to a traditionally black university."

"She can go to the community college right here. Ain't nothing wrong with dressing hair. You go off to college and you come back talking and acting like you white. Can't be proud of who you are."

The day turned. Junuh and Ruth had

built a large fire, hoping anyone out looking
would see it as a sign for help. As the lake
slowly drained, the sandbar once again became visible. They often searched the lake,
hoping to see some sign that Reese had made
it across. Junuh tuned the radio to a station
with weather reports, only to hear renewed
speculation that the storm might turn back
ashore.

He didn't want Ruth to hear this, didn't
even want to think about that possibility.

"Don't try to protect me," she scolded,
as he switched off the radio. "I have every
right to know."

"Right now, it seems to be a dice game."

"Crap shoot is the proper term."

"Crap shoot, whatever. I'm not a gam-
bler. I do know if that hurricane comes back
through here, we're in real trouble."

"Let's concentrate on the now. The now
is all of life that is real."

But the present would later fade from
Ruth's mind as she lay on the ground, watching clouds move through the tree boughs. The
effect was dreamy and calming and took her
back to a picnic years earlier.

*Frank dripped wine from the end of
his finger into Ruth's mouth. He had just
opened the second bottle. The dogwoods
were in bloom, the day especially warm; they
had seen a box turtle on the walk in. Duke
forest was huge and thick, and by getting just
a few yards off the trail, they could expect
total privacy.*

"I think I'm starting to love you, Ruth. I haven't told you that before."

"No, you haven't." Ruth's *mind was whirling. She knew she needed to respond.*

Frank was athletic and handsome. They both liked similar music and books. And now it was happening again, that fear she felt first as an ache in her belly that traveled up until the back of her throat felt cold. She remembered being on the lake as a child with her mother and father, and how perfect that was, innocent and trusting beyond words.

"I don't know if it's love I feel for you, Frank, but it's more than 'like.' The more I'm with you, the more I want to be with you."

Frank had taken some wine into his mouth then and kissed her, letting it wash around their tongues. Within minutes, most of their clothes had been removed, Ruth scissored one of his legs with both of hers, pressing her loins against his warm flesh. She felt his erection grow; her nipples ached they were so hard, and right in the middle of such passion the fear began, as it so often did. And once the fear began, she knew that the rest would just be going through the motions, the practiced dance, rote. Ruth could moan and arch her back, grip tightly, and scream when the time came to scream, but she was acting. Along with loving someone came losing him, and though she had spent thousands of dollars in therapy, she could not practice what she preached. She could not give herself and open those inner doors. Rather the reverse happened. A heavy gate closed at the opening to her heart and to her uterus, her warm, inner waters flowing in reverse against the struggling sperm, washing them toward bright, killing daylight. With each man, the relationship began dying at that moment; Ruth focused on his flaws, ignored his virtues, and in a day, or a week, or a month had convinced herself that the man was not worth the investment.

With female lovers, Ruth was able to relax more, knowing the woman was unable to instill in her the potential for the greatest loss. With imagery and dammed-up passion, she was able to hump her way to thundering orgasms, but Ruth quickly tired of a lover who could only make her body feel good and not father a child for her. And the years spun by, and lovers came and went, and Ruth cried each month when she noticed blood on the toilet tissue.

Ruth's mind came back from her daydream. "Junuh, I'm going to meditate down by the water."

"Just keep an eye cracked for any of our legless friends."

"You don't have to worry. I don't think I'm ever going to watch another episode of "Crocodile Hunter" again. Ruth chose a spot of sand that was clean and dry in the shade of a willow tree. She sat down and folded her legs into the lotus position.

Ruth closed her eyes and began to take deep breaths through her nose and out her mouth. She began her system of relaxation, of counting while white light slowly consumed each molecule of her body, the light insulating her until she no longer felt or heard the outside world, a white, warm blanket under which she was very safe.

Spirit Mother come to me. Bring your healing light. Take me far away from danger and pain. Deliver us all from strong winds and floods and famine, for you are our mother and we, your children.

Draw the breath in slowly, hold it and let it out, inhale again. Let go the sound of that crow calling, ignore it. The crow is not part of my special world. Ignore the wind in the trees. Ignore Junuh coughing. Expel any thoughts of Reese. Breathe in and out slowly, slowly. Nothing is in my special world but peace and white light. Feel the tension go, beginning in my neck. All the tension is leaving my body and I am at peace. Wonderful, blissful peace.

Whenever she meditated, Ruth always felt the tingle begin at her forehead and quickly flow down her face and neck. In only a couple of minutes the tingle was all the way to her feet. She felt especially happy and at peace there in the light world where nothing harmful could touch her. Meditating by the lake was much easier without the sirens and telephones of the city. She heard what she took to be the far-off hum of a jetliner, but was able to keep the noise at bay with deep breaths. One deep breath after another.

"Ruth, it's a boat!" Junuh yelled from the campsite, tearing her from her peaceful state. "Wave it down!"

Bright light flooded Ruth's eyes and

she was confused by the sudden interruption, but halfway across the lake, a boat was speeding past, its engine leaving a white wake.

Ruth jumped up, both arms in the air. "Hey!" she yelled. "Help us!"

Junuh was now nearby, jumping up and down on the sand, yelling and waving both arms. He launched himself into the edge of the water, making as much commotion as possible, but the boat didn't vary its course.

"You didn't see it coming, Ruth!"

"I heard something, but I thought it was an airplane, Junuh. I was meditating."

"You were meditating and let a motor boat ride right by!"

"I'm so sorry, Junuh. God, I'm sorry."

Junuh flopped down in the sand and watched the receding boat. "Maybe they'll see Reese, or make a second round."

But the boat quickly disappeared from sight, the sound of its motor fading to silence.

"I'm so sorry, Junuh."

Reese had not seen or heard the boat. For nearly an hour he slept, exhausted by his near drowning.

White caps roughened the lake's surface. Reese eased his legs back into the water. Any forward progress was going to take hard paddling. The water was deep out this far. Far across the lake, he could see something shining and hoped it to be the windshield of his truck. That would be his beacon, his light house. His prize for all this fear and discomfort would be to put his hand upon the sun-warmed hood of his Chevy.

Reese heard the whine of a jet and caught a glimpse of an airliner traveling east, probably gaining altitude from RDU Airport in route to Europe. He wondered if the captain had to change his route because of the storm, if the passengers could already see the pinwheel of the hurricane, tendrils spread like the arms of some great octopus? Excited vacationers above the wind and the rain, their eyes on the horizon and a city out of sight with granite museums, home to famous statues, ancient arenas where men and animals fought and spilled their blood, and quaint restaurants that smelled of garlic and cheese. That was the romanticized foreign world people saw in travel books. From his time abroad, Reese remembered sheep dung and Arabs with bad teeth. The man in first class sipping a scotch and soda reading *Esquire* would not want to think about sheep dung or a man a mile below him clinging to logs, hungry, desparate, his destination a couple of miles away across choppy water where snakes, alligators, and mad raccoons abided, his fate uncertain.

Reese's cheek felt puffy and hot where the raccoon had bitten him. The bleeding had stopped, and he hoped the lack of blood would lessen the chance of another alligator attacking. His chest was rubbed raw from grinding against the bark as he did breast strokes. The inner skin of each thigh also was chaffed. He reckoned he'd give twenty dollars for a tube of Vaseline. Reese's neck muscles burned when he lifted his head to sight on the windshield's glint.

"I need to go there, Lord," he said aloud. "I'll gladly stand up from this log and walk there if it be your will. Otherwise, I pray you'll give me the strength to paddle this log. I pray the wind will die down. I pray that raccoon didn't have rabies. Amen."

Reese thought about how the wind could be help or hindrance. If only it were behind him, he'd reach the truck in no time. He'd been the last to agree to come on this trip, and did so against his better judgment. Raccoons attacking by water? Nothing made sense, and not one thing seemed to be going his way. He tried to release his anger by ignoring everything but his paddling. His bad luck, the pain, not to mention that God couldn't even see fit to make the wind blow to his back. He closed his eyes and concentrated on the warm sunshine on his face. See, the sun was shining. It could be raining right now. At least the sun was shining.

The sun had not been benevolent in Kuwait, unrelenting, creating heat so dry that it sucked sweat away before it had time to bead and run. Reese was talking to Brown, a skinny, shy guy from Ohio, who wore a cross around his neck and often read from his small Bible. *They'd been awake the entire night, had engaged in three intense firefights. Now his unit was awaiting orders, the men getting what rest they could. Reese used his helmet as a pillow.*

"What you reading, Brown?"

"Psalms. I need a little peace and comfort after last night."

"What's comforting about the Bible? All that killing and hell and brimstone. The preacher up there shouting used to scare me to death."

"The Bible isn't scary if you're right with the Lord. Hell is nothing to fear if you're saved."

"We sure gave them A-rabs hell last night, didn't we?" said Reese, trying to change the subject. "We sent about a hundred sand niggers straight to hell."

"You shouldn't talk that way, Turner. If it wasn't for the grace of God, we could have been the ones hit."

"I don't know about the grace of God. I do know you're mighty fast with that laser sight. Faster than the rag heads are."

"That's the grace of God. The Lord sometimes works in ways we don't understand."

"I understand it. We're the American good guys and they're the sheep fucking, raghead infidels. God likes us the best."

Reese jerked his eyes open, momentarily confused by the haunting dreams that had frequently pushed him to the fringes of insanity, and the harsh reality of his current situation. His face was hot, seared by the strong sunlight, and he splashed water on it. When he raised his head to sight in on the distant windshield, his neck hurt all the way to the middle of his back. The sun had moved, and he saw only a faint glimmer from his goal. He forced himself to keep his head up to study the far shoreline for landmarks in case he lost the windshield glimmer. He marked tall pines side-by-side, taller than the hardwoods, resembling a gate.

Lowering his head, he checked his progress against the moss-hung cypress. Unless there was more than one, he hadn't made fifty yards in the past two hours.

"God, I believe I have the faith to move mountains in your name. I pray that this wind reverse and push me across this lake. I ask this in the name of Jesus Christ."

Picturing a giant hand pushing him across the lake, Reese put renewed energy into his paddling. He hammered the water, trying to rinse the terrible smells and sounds from the recesses of his mind.

Reese's inner arms were raw and stinging from rubbing against the log. His neck muscles were cramping. Although the stiff wind against his face felt good, it was the wind that was keeping him from making progress. Reese felt hot anger at the weakness within that he so often was forced to combat.

I could propel this log like a power boat if I just had the faith, Reese thought. I could stand up from here and walk. I could run to that truck. If Satan wasn't so strong and I wasn't so weak....

He pummeled the water for about a minute until he was gasping for breath and his shoulders screamed with pain. He stopped, his shame manifested in tears.

"I believe, Lord," he cried. "Help me." His chest heaved. "I love you, God, and Satan, I hate you, you beast. You bastard, killing SOB. I hate you." His voice was loud upon the water. "I hate you, Satan, you god-damned bastard, son of a fucking whore. You god-damned shit-eating fucker. I hate you, Satan."

His tears turned into a sob. "Forgive my weakness, Lord. I'm not talking about you. It's Satan, the son-of-a-bitch. If I was just stronger. God-damned Satan — you have damned him, Lord, but I can't escape his hooks, or I'd stand up from here and walk. I ain't cussing you, Lord. God-damn him, I ain't cussing you, Lord. I ain't cussing you. I'm just weak."

Reese mopped the wound on his cheek, then he took several long, slow breaths as he sighted on the small gleam that still offered guidance.

"Hear me God. I'm going across this lake. Your servant, Reese Turner, is crossing this lake, and the Devil ain't holding me back. Not if it's a matter of faith. Your disciple, your humble servant is crossing this lake 'cause I believe, and the *Bible* says I only have to believe."

Reese kicked water until it turned white, pulled water with his arms as the raw sores on his chest ground against the bark of the logs, and recited another prayer through gritted teeth.

"Though I have walked in the shadow of death and seen the gross and the tormented with my own eyes, I am not troubled.

147

I've carried this weight around my neck till the bones ground to dust under it, but I have not asked to put it down. You, Lord, said, 'Believe in me, and I will not put that one more ounce upon you that breaks your back,' and though I have felt my spine at the snapping point it did not. It did not because I believed, and I believe now, and I will not give up until I am across that lake, because I have brethren dependant on me now. Weak, lost people not knowing of the Lord."

Reese fought the water, kicking and grabbing it until his effort was even greater than the wind that sought to defeat him, and he began to inch forward across the lake, passing the moss-covered tree. He was strengthened by the knowledge of his progress, and he fought even harder, sucking the pungent air in great draughts. Blood from his chest trickled down both sides of the raft.

"The power and the glory, God Almighty, and you said to a boy whose people were tormented by a giant to go before his foe with a slingshot and a stone, and the boy did so with you in his heart, and he slew the giant, and I am your servant, and you delivered me alone from that burning cauldron of death when I did not even know your name, and now as your servant I call for the wind to stop and you have put your hand upon the Devil's hot mouth and stopped his breath, and I sing the praises of a man once bound for hell and now assured a place in heaven. Hallelujah!"

For nearly an hour Reese cursed life,

praised heaven and worked so hard that he was greater than the wind, and the raft slipped toward the opposite bank, while the sun slid down the horizon toward nightfall, Reese's heat becoming a fever that radiated from the wound where the raccoon's fangs had pierced him. As the day diminished, his efforts to propel the craft became less strong, then meager, and his eyes finally closed as he fell into exhausted, fevered sleep.

Then the wind changed, drying the sweat on Reese's back, and like the flicker of small tongues, soothing his wounds. Near midnight, with the lake lit by waning moonlight, the raft bumped into a log that jutted into the water along the far shore.

The raft bobbled only a few yards from Reese's pickup truck, unscathed from the storm. For nearly an hour the raft nudged the bottom as Reese slept. Then a new breath of wind arose and mounted until the raft began to drift away from the hard-earned shore.

As white caps grew, Reese and the raft were pushed slowly but steadily back across the lake. When the eastern sky began to show pink, the raft drifted into the calm water of the cove where Ruth and Junuh lay shivering by gray coals at the campsite.

Ruth was dreading to move her aching joints when a flight of geese landed on the lake, then quickly took flight, honking in alarm. Ruth rose up on one elbow to see what had spooked the geese. There, gently bobbing in the shallow water beyond the sandbar was Reese, motionless on his narrow raft.

"Wake up, Junuh! Get up quick."

Junuh came up from the ground as if jerked with a rope. "Are there snakes again?" He rubbed his eyes. "What's the matter?"

"Look, it's Reese. I think he's unconscious."

In just moments, Ruth and Junuh were knee-deep in water bending over Reese. His face was swollen, the skin stretched tight and red. He had a fever. He moaned, then opened his eyes and looked wildly about as the two lifted him from the raft and half-carried, half-dragged him to the fire.

Chapter 8

Junuh and Ruth put Reese on the sleeping bag beside the fire. His face was sunburned, chaffed and swollen from the raccoon bite. Reese began mumbling within minutes, then as Ruth was mopping his face, he bolted upright and tried to stand.

"Easy Reese," Junuh said, holding his arm. "Go slow. You need to rest, buddy. You've been through an ordeal."

"Where is my truck?"

"Your truck is across the lake."

"No, I was right at it. I could read the license plate."

"All I know, Reese, is you got out of sight on the lake, but you were here in the cove this morning."

"God took me across that lake. I know he did. I could nearly touch my pickup."

"How did you get this wound on your face?"

"A raccoon. Acted crazy. Got on the raft with me. An alligator ate it."

Junuh cut his eyes at Ruth. "A raccoon attacked you, and an alligator ate the raccoon?"

"Yeah. Raccoon bit my face. He was probably rabid. Then an alligator ate him."

"That sounds crazy, Reese," Ruth said.

"You think I'm lying? Why come you think they call this Alligator Lake?"

"I'm just glad you're back," Ruth said. "You look like you've been in a battle."

"I was. Me against the Devil. I think he won this round, but the war ain't over. Not by a long shot."

Not much time passed before Reese's breath stretched out, becoming long and peaceful. He slept for hours.

Son arrived when Ruth was passing around chunks of venison. He stepped from his boat with a basket in one hand, its contents covered by a towel. In his other arm he carried another watermelon.

"Welcome," Ruth said. "We were just about to eat. You're welcome to join us."

Son stepped closer to the fire. He had changed clothes, but his pants were wet to the knees. Junuh offered him a chunk of meat. "You did the hard part. You should have taken some of the meat with you."

Son reached for it, sniffed it, then took a tentative bite, chewing slowly, as if in judgment.

"How's your boat floating?" Reese asked.

"Reparation. A repairing or being repaired."

"I know. From *Webster's*," Reese said. "Your boat looks pretty swamped. How'd you get here without sinking?"

"Paradise is not far."

"This paradise. Tell me about it."

"A place or state of bliss, felicity, or delight."

Reese rolled his shoulders. "Man, you have a one-track mind."

"Is paradise your home?" Ruth asked.

Son nodded.

"Where is it?"

Son pointed away from the direction they had come to the lake.

"Is there a telephone in paradise?" Junah asked.

Son shook his head.

"Is there a car or truck maybe?"

He shook his head again, then popped the remainer of the meat into his mouth.

"Where's your family?" Ruth asked.

Son touched the middle of his chest. "My heart, the trees, the water, the sky. Merrie said she would be there."

"Who's Mary?" Reese asked?

"Mother."

"Your mother's name is Mary!"

Son nodded.

"What's your father's name?" Reese asked.

"My father is God."

Reese raised both arms and slowly shook his head. The son of God and Mary who wants us to follow him to paradise. Junuh, you sure autistic is the right word? What about schizophrenic?"

"Hush!" Ruth scolded. Junuh didn't answer.

"Schizophrenia, a psychotic disorder characterized by loss of contact with the environment..."

"What does *Webster's* say about nut?" Reese asked, interrupting.

"Shut up, Reese," Ruth commanded. "Don't pay any attention to him, Son. How long have you lived by the lake?"

"Always."

Ruth nodded. "Okay. Where and when were you born?"

"I was born in paradise. I was born on June the sixth, nineteen-sixty-nine. Gemini. The third sign of the zodiac."

Reese stood suddenly and walked away from the fire, turning his back on the others.

From the basket, Son produced a quart jar of honey and a loaf of bread, pie-shaped and very brown. Junuh remembered his mother making bread like that in the thick, cast-iron dutch oven on top of the stove. Son also had brought another chicken, this one gutted, cleaned and ready to be cooked. He handed the food to Ruth.

"Oh, my goodness! Thank you!" Reese still had his back turned. "Reese, look. Watermelon. Honey and home-baked bread. And a chicken that is so clean it puts the one you cleaned to shame, Junuh. A feast!"

Reese continued to stare toward the water. "Did you make this honey, Son?"

"The bees did. Honey, a thick viscid material elaborated out of the nectar of flowers in the honey sac of various bees. The bees made the honey."

"I know, but are they your bees?"

Son nodded. "*Genesis* 1:28: 'Be fruitful and multiply, and replenish the earth, and subdue it: And have dominion over the fish of the sea, and over the fowl of the air, and over every living thing that moveth upon the earth.'"

"Well, thank your bees for us," Ruth said. "This is truly a wonderful meal."

Son bent over and scooped up a palmful of sand, dribbling it slowly between his fingers, concentrating on how the grains fractured and reflected the light. He bent a second time, and when he did, his necklace swung from beneath his shirt, a simple ornament, half a clam shell suspended from a strip of rawhide. The outer edge of the shell was shiny with lacquer, the concave interior much more spectacular, deep purple, imbedded with clear crystals. The jewels caught the light from the campfire and blazed like a universe unto itself.

Junuh's breath caught when he saw the ornament. His eyes fastened on the fire inside the shell. "Your necklace. Where does it come from?"

Son finished dribbling the sand. "Merrie made it. She told me if I was ever in a place where you can't see the night sky, just look here."

"It's a beautiful piece of jewelry."

Junuh suddenly felt as if he were standing on the edge of a great cliff. The jeweled shell had such depth and distance that he felt as if he might step off the precipice and fall forever through a maze of stars.

"Merrie lives there now. There are no

storms." Son tucked the shell back within his shirt. Junuh felt himself returning to solid footing. Son picked up another handful of sand. "Tomorrow we go to paradise. The storm will come tomorrow."

Reese turned around, his face mottled by shadows from the dancing fire. "What do you know about this storm?"

"A big storm. I've got to find Dorothy. Help me find Dorothy."

"How do you know about this storm?" Reese asked.

"Merrie tells me."

"Your dead mother tells you?"

"Energy only changes form. Merrie is still Merrie. Paradise is safe from storms."

"What's the problem with your boat?" Junuh asked. "Maybe we can help you fix it. We'll pay you good to carry us across that lake."

Son shook his head. "Time, the measured or measurable period during which an action, process, or condition exists or continues. Faulkner wrote *The Sound and the Fury*; before that, Hemingway wrote, *The Sun Also Rises*. We've got to get home, Toto. I think there's a twister coming."

Reese rolled his eyes. "Thanks for the honey and the bread, Mister. The watermelon. You get your boat fixed and want to make some cash, come on by. Otherwise, why don't you stay in paradise. We'll be all right."

"Reese! He's trying to help us," Ruth said. "You shouldn't be so rude."

Son turned abruptly and disappeared as soundlessly as he had appeared. Ruth poured honey on a chunk of bread and passed it to Junuh. She did the same for Reese, then prepared a piece for herself. They ate hungrily, licking their fingers clean. Junuh turned on the radio, and they listened to the latest version of the weather, signs indicating more and more that the storm would come back ashore. Junuh stared intently across the lake. Reese studied him for a moment.

"You're looking pretty serious, Doc. Did the swamp man spook you, too?"

"I don't understand why you're so afraid of Son," Ruth said to Reese. "All he tries to do is help us."

"First of all, I'm not afraid of him," Reese replied. "And you're a bleeding heart liberal, Ruth. You mean well, but there are evils in this world you have no concept of. You think the whole world is sugar and pie, and it ain't. I've seen the other side."

"Don't sell me short, Reese. I work with death every day. My personal life — believe me, it ain't sugar and pie. I don't think there is any reason for us to be so damn wary of a man who has shown nothing but good intentions since he arrived."

"What's your honest opinion of him, Doc? Don't you think he's nuts?"

Junuh gazed into the fire. "He's autistic, that's evident. Actually, I think he is highly intelligent; he's a walking encyclopedia. I think he's basically harmless though, but as we all know, he doesn't hesitate to kill."

"What about this paradise thing?" Reese asked.

157

"That, I'm not sure about. He lives somewhere. He gets supplies. He's got to know how to get out of this swamp."

"But, he talks so crazy, Doc. Says he's the son of God."

"He was talking in symbolism," Ruth said. "We are all the children of God."

Reese leaned forward and hugged his knees. "What about his birthday?"

"What about it?" Ruth answered.

"June sixth, nineteen-sixty-nine. June's the sixth moth. That's more sixes than I like to see."

Junuh glanced up sharply at Reese. Ruth looked confused. "So, what's the deal with sixes?" she asked. "Is this some Southern thing?"

"It's a Biblical thing," Reese said. "You know it, Doc. Tell her."

"Six-six-six, it's the mark of the beast. From *Revelation*. Supposedly, in the future, after the rapture, all people will be forced to wear the numbers six-six-six. If you don't wear the numbers, you die physically. If you do wear them, you die spiritually."

"Big deal," Ruth said. "A few million other people were born on that day. Let's get serious. There's a hurricane out there. You're the one acting paranoid now, Reese."

"I just find it odd," Reese said. "Guy wants us to follow him to paradise, and he's born under the sign of the beast."

"Or, a guy was born on June sixth, and he brings us food and wants to take us to a safe place when a hurricane is coming. I believe in a benevolent God, Reese. So did Nate.

That's what brings us here."

"Yeah? And Nate is dead, and we're stranded in a swamp, and I may have been bitten by a rabid raccoon yesterday. And a category-four hurricane is about to swallow us. God is benevolent. He also expects people to help themselves."

Junuh busied himself snapping more green wood to put into the fire. He wrestled with his thoughts. Finally, he spoke. "That necklace he was wearing, did either of you notice it?"

"The shell?" Ruth asked.

"Yeah, the shell."

"What about it?"

"Nate told me about a visitor he had sometimes at night," Junah said. "I think he was hallucinating, but he told me a man came to visit him at night."

Reese nodded. "He told me about him. I told him he was dreaming."

"Once, he said the man showed him a necklace he wore," Junuh continued. "A half shell on a strip of leather with stars inside. Son's necklace looked exactly like that. I had the strangest feeling when I saw it."

"Half the hippies in the world have a shell or some beads strung around their necks."

"Yeah, but Nate didn't have some wandering hippie in his room. I just had the strangest feeling when I saw it. Kind of like *deja vu*."

"We have to get off this lake," Reese said. "We're all starting to get a little nuts."

"What if we went with him?" Junuh

said. What if we went to his house, or camp, or whatever he lives in? There's got to be a path or road that leads to civilization."

"Or a path that leads to hell," Reese replied. "There's evil in this world. Evil that you two don't want to admit exists. Satan walks in many forms."

"Reese, you make me sick," Ruth said. "Son is just a man who wants to help us. He's not evil. I'm not sure that evil even exists. Just a lack of goodness. Nate didn't die from evil overtaking him. There just wasn't enough goodness to save him." She hugged her knees. "I think we are all out here together for some good reason. I think Nate brought us all here. He knew something we didn't."

"I don't see good reason in a category-four hurricane. If that thing comes ashore, people, we're goners. Drowning ain't pretty."

"Then we go with Son."

"What if this is a test of faith?" Reese said. "We're tempted to do the easy thing, instead of relying on God to protect us."

"You keep forgetting, Reese," Ruth said. "We're not of your congregation. We don't believe the same."

"Then maybe it is high time you started believing."

Dusk fell quickly in the heavy air of August. Insects came in droves and owls hooted. But the night sounds were not as thick as they had been when the three first came to the lake, as if the animals and bugs sensed a disturbance in the atmosphere and had gone inland to higher and dryer ground.

The chicken sizzled on the spit as the three finished the bread and honey and ate the watermelon to the rind.

Junuh was especially quiet. He left the fire and walked to the edge of the water. He thought about the boat that had passed earlier that day, of how different things might be now if they had been spotted. Or, if Reese had made it across the lake on the raft. Or, if Son had been a regular fellow who just happened to live on the lake. He thought about the hurricane forecast for tomorrow and wondered if they could live through a direct hit. Water and storms had taken everyone who had died in his family. No one ever found the bodies of his mother and father. Crabs and fish probably had eaten them. Junuh knew that his father would have liked the irony of that, but his mother would have preferred a coffin buried in a spot beside her eldest son.

Junuh spied the bottle bobbing a couple of yards off the end of the sandbar. Only the neck protruded from the water, and Junuh wondered what the bottle might contain — possibly a message. He and Cleo often had sent messages to sea in bottles. None ever had been answered.

The bottle was balanced upright because it was almost full of red wine. Junuh lifted it and read the label — Richard's Four Roses, an inexpensive fortified wine that was mostly consumed by hard-core alcoholics because it was strong and cheap. He held the bottle up to the sky — three-quarters full;

the cap was screwed tight. Probably lost recently in the lake by fishermen, could have
even washed into the lake on one of the swollen creeks.

Junuh remembered tasting a similar
wine once many years ago. His father had
been good for a drunk about twice a year,
and when it came, the cause was a similar
red wine that left him sleeping on the porch
in a pool of puke. Once, he left a couple of
fingers of wine in the bottle, and Junuh took
a big gulp, only to spew it from his mouth in
a red mist. He wondered how his father, or
any human, could find pleasure in such an
acid taste, and what that taste did to a man.
How it made him laugh and dance at first,
then lie down, unable to rise, and puke.

Junuh was about to heave the bottle
far into the lake when the memory of two
black winos outside of Well Spring Grocery
popped into his mind. Just a couple of days
ago when he was picking up some things for
the camping trip. The two men looked to be
in their late forties and were resting on a
sheet of cardboard in the shade of a tree
outside the store, propped up on their elbows
and talking to whoever looked their way.

*"Hey home," one of the men said to
Junuh. "How 'bout a dollar for a brother?"*

*Junuh didn't look at the men as he
entered the store, didn't answer, or acknowl-
edge their existence.*

*He took his time loading a cart, debat-
ing which foods to take on a three-day expe-*

dition to the woods. When he came back outside, the two winos were still on their bed of
cardboard. Both keyed on Junuh. "Blood,
what you got in that sack for me?"

Junuh didn't answer, stared straight
ahead. The wino who had spoken looked at
his buddy. "Nigger can't hear. Hey, homie,
throw me an apple."

"All I have are kiwi fruit."

"Kiwi fruit? Niggers don't eat kiwi fruit.
They eat apples. Apples and Richard's wine.
Bet 'ya ain't got any Richard's in that sack."

"Shit, blood, that store don't stock no
Richard's. Just kiwi fruit and stuff for white
people and Oreos like we got here."

Junuh was even with the men. He
picked up his stride, his eyes set on his Volvo
sedan. "Hey, Uncle Tom, give a nigger a dollar. You got a dollar I know damn well. Got
two dollars."

Several white shoppers were skirting
the little drama that was developing, faces
straight ahead, smiles set. Junuh had passed
the men now. Their words slammed into his
back.

"Little faggot ignore us. Go home to his
sweet little apartment. Probably got him a
white girlfriend — or boyfriend. Boyfriend
more like it. Him and his boyfriend stick them
kiwi fruit up their butts. Listen to BB King on
the CD player. Me and Otis, we living the
blues. And the blacks. Living the blues and
the blacks and hustling us some Richard's and
ain't 'shamed of shit. Why you so 'shamed,
boy? Man 'shamed of his own kind...."

Junuh slammed his car door harder

*than usual to stop the men's voices. When
he started the engine, the sounds of NPR filled
the interior.*

Junuh lowered his arm. With deliberation, he unscrewed the cap and held it in his
free hand. With even more deliberation, he
turned the bottle up and drank a long swallow before his taste buds had a chance to
kick in. When he did taste the wine, his stomach heaved for a moment, but he held it down
— acrid, sickly sweet, but not altogether unpleasant. To tell the truth, straight bourbon
tasted worse. Junuh turned the bottle up
again, a strange excitement he never had
experienced flowing through his cells.

Reese noticed that Junuh excused himself several times as darkness was descending over the campsite. He always went down
to the sandbar. The chicken was beginning
to sizzle over the fire, and Junuh kept ad-
justing the way the bird hung over the coals.
"Gonna cook this chicken just right,"
he said. "Wish we had a frying pan and some
lard. Can't nobody cook chicken like black
people."
Reese raised one eyebrow at Ruth. "You
ain't never fried a chicken in your life, Doc."
"The shit you preach," Junuh an-
swered. "There's a lot about me you don't
know."
Reese chuckled. He'd never heard
Junuh talk so openly. "You're the chicken

man, Doc. You cook it and I'll eat it."

Junuh narrowed his eyes at Reese. "Chicken man. You ain't calling me scared, are you, Preacherman?"

"Naw. Not at all. I just meant if you say you know how to cook chicken, I believe you."

"Just checking. I don't take to being called chicken. Especially by white people."

Wrinkles furrowed Reese's brow. "Didn't mean it that way at all, Junuh."

"Just checking. Just checking." Junuh stumbled once as he set off for the sandbar again.

Reese stared at Ruth. "What's with him? He knew what I was saying."

"We're all stressed out," Ruth replied. "I feel like a wound guitar string myself."

When Junuh returned, he was carrying the wine bottle by the neck. It was about half full. He sat down heavily, then opened the bottle and drank a large belt. Ruth's eyes were large as she stared. Reese studied the label from his distance. He knew the wine well, had drunk his share of the potent stuff in his bad days.

"Dadgum, Doc," Reese said. "Winos call that stuff 'the blood.' Where'd you get that?"

"Washed in on the flood. I couldn't see any sense in letting it go to waste. I don't sense an objection, do I?"

"No. Other than I think drinking to abuse is a sin. I can't say I've never drunk it. Got my share of hangovers, too. I just didn't think you were much of a drinker. Richard's is pretty hard-core stuff."

"Want a swallow?"

"No. Thank you, though. My drinking days are behind me, thank the Lord."

"How 'bout you, Ruth? Want a nip to warm 'ya?"

"No, thank you, Junuh."

"You don't drink with black people?"

"Junuh, that's ridiculous. I'm just not in the mood for wine right now. Don't drink with black people? Half my friends are black." Ruth stared at Reese. Her face was dark with concern. "If I had a bottle of Champagne, I don't think I could drink a drop right now. I guess it's a blessing, but I've never been able to drink while in a dark mood."

"Well, you implying that I'm a wino? That I wouldn't be drinking right now if I wasn't a drunk?"

Ruth fluttered one hand in the air like a bird. "What in the world has gotten into you, Junuh? I'm not implying anything." Ruth's mouth hung open.

"Yeah, yeah. Just checking." Junuh took another pull from his bottle, then capped it. He got to his feet and went to the fire. Using a stick, he poked the chicken several times, then stood staring at it.

"I guess ya'll blame me for all this." A deep sadness was etched in Junuh's face.

"Blame you for what?" Reese asked.

"Being in this predicament. Out here on this lake in the first place. Letting Nate die."

"Daggone, Junuh," Reese said. "I was his preacher. Direct line to the Lord, and he died."

166

"Yeah, and I gave him most of his chemo treatments," Ruth said. "It had nothing to do with you, Junuh. You're a good doctor. I see that every day."

Walking back to the wine bottle, Junuh trod flat-footed and heavy. He rolled to his back as he sat down, then rose, uncapped the bottle and took another long swallow.

"You might go easy, Doc," Reese said. "That stuff will make you crazy. Believe me. I know through first-hand experience."

"Maybe I'm tougher than you, Preacherman. You stop and consider that? I was raised hard. Wasn't given nothing. My daddy drank this kind'a wine. Maybe I was just born tougher than you. A preacherman. Makes his living with words. I been scrambling since I started breathing. That's what it is to be black."

Ruth fluttered her hand with frustration. "Why all this sudden racial talk, Junuh? I know there are differences between the three of us, but color hasn't been an issue."

Junuh showed his palm. I ain't accusing nobody. Just stating some facts. You ain't feeling no guilt, are 'ya, Miss Ruth?"

"No! Absolutely not."

"Good. The truth will set you free."

Junuh drank from his bottle again. Reese watched his Adam's apple rise and fall. Fortified wine. Liquid crack, some people called it. Reese shuddered as he remembered the exact taste and smell of the wine, how it could turn a good man into a stumbling, fighting, babbling idiot in an hour's time. He knew Junuh needed some food in his belly.

167

"That chicken about ready?" Reese asked. "I'm getting pretty hungry myself."

Junuh heaved to his feet. "I'm the chicken man. Can't no white people cook chicken right." Flames jumped from the coals when Junuh poked the bird and fat dripped into the fire. "'Bout there. Few more minutes." Junuh returned to his seat. Taking another long swallow, he stared for a time at the quickly darkening lake. "Tomorrow this time, it'll all be over. Storm either come or it don't. I drown or I don't. Serve me right if I drown. Let my own mama and daddy drown in a storm. I couldn't be bothered to come get them. Scared I might not look professional enough if I miss a reception. Let my mama and daddy drown like dogs."

Junuh bubbled the wine again. Reese shuddered. "Junuh, I ain't trying to mess with your business, but you ought to pour out the rest of that wine. You're going to be sick as a dog if you don't."

"I'm a doctor, ain't I? I know about being sick. 'Less you don't think I'm much of a doctor."

"And you're starting to act like a drunk, wanting to argue and make a scene. I've done the same thing. Why don't you let me get you some chicken. Tomorrow is going to be a busy day."

Reese stood and walked toward the fire. Junuh collapsed once before he was able to get to his feet. He met Reese at the fire. "Just chill, Preacherman. I'm cooking this bird. Serve you up hot in about five minutes."

"I'm just trying to help, Junuh. I'm not

trying to take over. But that alcohol is working on you."

"You can help me by sitting down and letting me cook."

Junuh turned from Reese. He jabbed the chicken with his stick, but too hard this time, and the spit came off the support. The chicken dropped into the coals. Junuh reached for it, ignoring the heat. The leg he grabbed came loose from the body, and the chicken fell back into the coals, now blazing from the fat. Ruth stood, uncertain what to do. Reese just watched as Junuh destroyed their supper. Junuh wiped his hand on his pants, fumbled in his pocket, and withdrew his Swiss Army knife. He opened a blade and jabbed repeatedly at the burning bird, but it kept falling off.

"Let me see that knife..." Reese said. Junuh whirled toward him, the tip of the blade pointed at Reese's face. Standing splay-legged, Junuh swayed slightly, a hollow, bitterness in his eyes that Reese had seen in few men. Reese raised both hands, palms out and stepped backward.

"Okay, you got it," he said. "I'll just get out of your way."

Ruth jumped between the two men, her face a mask of grim defiance. She grabbed the stick Junuh had been using, stuck it through the chicken and lifted it from the coals. She laid the carcass in one of the salvaged pans. "You — over there," she said to Junuh. "You — over there," she told Reese, as if they were two young boys on the threshold of a fistfight. Without words, the men returned to their seats. Ruth began brushing gray ash and burned skin from the chicken. Junuh dove back into his bottle, taking a long swallow that left only about three fingers of wine remaining.

"I'm sorry, ya'll. I'm sorry." He stared at the remaining wine, then slung the bottle toward the lake. It splashed in the darkness. "I'm empty as that bottle inside. It's all used up. Spent my heritage, everything I was raised to know running from it. Changed my voice. Forgot my history. Tried to be some kind'a man who can't be — not white, not black." Junuh snorted and wiped his eyes. Reese drew in the dirt with his finger. Ruth continued to pick at the chicken, but her eyes were on Junuh.

"This hurricane. It's coming for me. I let my mama and daddy drown 'cause I wasn't any kind'a man. I'm gonna drown tomorrow like a mad dog, and there won't be five people who care. Don't nobody know me, and I don't know me. Don't know my own damn self."

"God knows you," Reese said. "He knows you as a son, Junuh."

"Too late for that."

"I know you, Junuh," Ruth said. "I know you, and I admire you."

"Naw, naw." Junuh rolled to his back. His breathing was labored. After a minute, he rolled to his stomach and puked up a red pool of liquid. Ruth was immediately at his side.

"Let it all come up, Junuh. Get all that poison out of your body." She kneaded his shoulder. Another gush of vomit came from

170

his mouth. He moaned. Ruth rubbed his forehead as his breathing went long and deep and he slowly fell into sleep.

"He's gonna feel like crap in the morning" Reese said. "Believe me, 'cause I been there."

"What in the world was he drinking? I've never seen anyone change personalities so thoroughly. My God, Reese. He pulled a knife on you."

Reese chuckled. "You call that a knife? In my life, I've come in contact with some rough guys, Ruth." He laughed. "A brand new Swiss Army knife, and he had the fingernail file open. I wasn't exactly in mortal danger."

Ruth smiled. "He scared me." She stroked his cheek. He's such a sweetheart. I've never seen anyone change so much from alcohol."

"Alcohol is one of the Devil's chief tools. As much as you dislike me, Ruth, you would have hated me tenfold when I drank."

"I don't dislike you, Reese. We just disagree on some things. At least you have opinions. I admire someone willing to stand up for what he believes."

The chicken was gritty, but Ruth and Reese ate it anyway. Junuh snored as he slept. Occasionally, he talked in his sleep, the words angry and unintelligible. "He's gonna have some kind of hangover when he wakes up," Reese said. "I bet he hadn't been drunk twice in his whole life."

"Junuh is carrying a lot of psychological baggage. He needs to be in therapy."

"He needs to be on his knees in prayer. That's what's wrong with Chapel Hill. Half the people there are in some type of therapy. Think they can pay their way out of their problems. Another man or woman can't forgive your sins. That comes from the Lord."

"Why are you so angry, Reese? When Junuh pointed his knife at you, your face, you looked like you wanted him to cut you. And if he had, I think you would have beaten him into the dirt. And you're a minister. But you seem to believe more in the *Old Testament* than the *New.* You're so combative. You have such a chip on your shoulder. Christ came to Earth in peace. You remind me of Job more than Christ. It's like you want to be hurt, just so you can prove yourself. There's nothing to prove. The universe is goodness, and our chore is to find out how we fit into that goodness. The whole universe is one big wonderful cathedral, but you try to package it into little conniving, spiteful, bitter prisons that a person has to escape. Don't you feel God when you see a flight of geese landing on the lake? Didn't you feel God when that hurricane was on top of us and we lived through it with hardly a scratch? Nate wasn't bitter when he was dying. He was looking out the window and smiling and beckoning for someone to come inside the room. It was beautiful."

Reese tossed a chicken bone toward the black water. "We're born crying while our mothers scream," he said, "and we die hurting and scared. Nate was whacked out of his mind on narcotics when he died. I didn't see any beauty in it. But the *Bible* says have faith, so I do. Yesterday I tried to paddle across this lake. And I couldn't. I took my mustard seed of faith, and I must have needed a watermelon. I failed you and Junuh, and I failed God. I just wasn't strong enough. You're all the time telling me I should hear God in the wind and see him in falling stars. Well, maybe I don't so much, but I do see him in the pulse right here in my wrist. I hear him in that damn coughing I do because I'm drawing breath, even though I can't stop smoking cigarettes. You hug a tree and say you're flawless and guiltless and that evil is only imagined. I spit up phlegm every morning and ask God that I don't screw the world up any worse than I have already during the coming day, that I have the faith to stand up in front of people and say, 'Look at me — and God still allows me to draw breath.'"

Reese took a deep, long breath, and a single sob jerked his shoulders. Quickly, he wiped the corner of his eye. Ruth rested her forehead against her knees for several moments. Her eyes were shiny when she lifted her face.

"I guess you consider me to be a total infidel."

"I think you're lost," Reese answered. "But you're certainly not too late to be saved. I wish I could take you down to that lake and baptize you in the name of Jesus Christ."

"And I wish that you and Junuh could hear the whisper of the Holy Spirit in the hoot of that owl we just heard," Ruth replied.

"I wish that too. I wish the road was that smooth and simple."

"Tell me about the war, Reese."

"There's not much to tell."

"The owl tells me there is."

Reese sucked in his breath again, lowered his head. Interlocking his fingers, he masked his nose and eyes. "You want to hear about the war. Do you despise me for that, too?"

"I'm sorry for what you had to go through, but I admire you for answering the call to duty. I never blamed soldiers for following orders, just the governments that created the orders. Was it a terrible experience?"

Reese said nothing for nearly a minute. He cleared his throat a couple of times, then spoke, still not looking at Ruth. "I was one big screw-up throughout my teenage years. Didn't care about nothing but getting high. I wasn't close to my parents or my little sister. I made grades just good enough to keep me in school so I could sell a little pot between classes and smoke for free."

"I did my share of drugs, too, Reese."

"It was like I didn't want to feel anything. I just wanted to be numb. I'd spend the whole weekend in my room with the door locked and a set of headphones on. I didn't care anything about sports. Ate nothing but junk food. I'd sit up till three A.M. watching TV."

An explosion of water came from the lake, and a chorus of scared, honking geese filled the night air. Ruth scooted closer to the fire.

"Alligator or large snapping turtle,"
Reese explained.

"Didn't your parents get on your case?"
Ruth asked. "My parents both died young,
but they knew everything I did."

"They were both alcoholics. As long as
I didn't get into their gin and tonic fixings, I
don't think they cared what I did." He looked
as if he were seeing pictures long submerged.
"But, yeah, my dad finally started getting on
my case and I just moved out, sold dope,
scrounged, wasted a few years. Then I joined
the Army on a whim. I didn't plan on Saddam
Hussein invading Kuwait. Six months after
boot camp, I was smack dab in the middle of
the a desert in southern Iraq. Radio operator
in an Abrams tank. Finest killing machine
ever made."

Taking out his pocket knife, Reese concentrated on cleaning under his thumb nail.
He opened and closed his mouth a couple of
times. "I – I've never talked to anyone about
this. Not except the Lord."

"I'm a good listener, Reese. I've always
felt like you had something inside you didn't
talk about. I could write a book with all the
little secrets I've stored away and let fester."

Reese cleared his throat, then spit toward the coals. "Our unit had already been
through several fire fights. We had several
enemy kills to our credit." He curled his finger through the chain that suspended his
cross. "We had gotten orders to stand down
that night — relax in civilian talk. I was on
radio watch, but I had switched off the tactical station and tuned in Oil Can Betty, this

propagandist woman on a station out of Baghdad. She was always talking this outrageous stuff about how our wives and girlfriends were cheating on us at home. A lot of people listened to her for kicks, but I shouldn't have been off the tactical frequency. All of a sudden, the alarm went off that we were in the radar sights of another tank. Everybody scrambled into action, and I switched to the tactical station and started broadcasting our position."

Reese stopped and took a long, deep breath. He pinched the bridge of his nose. His shoulders shook when he exhaled. The next second, a 120-millimeter round slammed into our tank. All I remember was fire and smoke and scrambling to get to the escape hatch. I got out but the rest of the crew didn't."

Reese twisted the chain around his finger. "It was friendly fire. One of our own tanks. Their operator said he tried to raise me on the hook. I lied and said I had interference."

"It sounds like the other tank was more at fault."

"Not really. We made split-second decisions all the time. If I had been on frequency, I'd have come back with code when he challenged me. I was goofing off, and three men died. I should have died, too. I just got some burns on my arms."

"Then consider yourself lucky. It's evident that God had work for you to do."

"But why me? There was this guy named Brown. Nice guy — he was always trying to convert me. This cross I wear — it was his. I remember they brought his body out of the tank, and laid it in the sand. I went over to him and said I was sorry. I took the cross from around his neck. I think he would have wanted me to have it."

"I thought that cross was special to you. You touch it often."

Reese uncurled the cross from his finger, as if only then aware of holding it. "I stayed drunk for the next two years. Drunk and high. I was just waiting to die. Finally, the Lord delivered me from my sins, and I've been preaching from rock walls or from behind the meat counter ever since. People think I'm crazy, but I feel directed by God."

Reese looked into Ruth's eyes for a moment, blinked, and glanced away from her toward the lake. "Tomorrow at daybreak, we need to start bushwhacking out of here. Forget about the truck, go straight east. We're probably not much more than a few miles from a road. We should have done that in the first place. Me and my leadership!" Sighing, he stood and walked until he was swallowed by the darkness beside the water.

Reese had prayed himself to sleep when he was startled by a hand on his shoulder. Instinctively, he jerked away from the touch.

"It's me," Ruth said. "I didn't mean to scare you."

"You didn't scare me." Reese touched his fingers to his inflamed cheek. "What are you doing out here?"

"Checking on you. I drifted off to sleep,

then woke up and realized you hadn't come back. You ought to come back to the fire."

"The fire is too hot."

"It keeps the mosquitoes away."

"I've been bitten so many times now I don't even feel them."

Ruth sat with her legs curled under her. The moon shone through a break in the clouds, the white light off the lake illuminating Reese's form, almost like a halo. "I wanted to apologize mostly, for all the arguing I've done over the last few days. We shouldn't be arguing. Especially with things as they are."

Reese was silent for several seconds. "I'm sorry if I offended you. I've never been very good at listening to people."

"Well, I've probably listened too much of my life. I never thought I had anything worth saying."

"You're one of the most intelligent people I've ever met," Reese said. "I envy your trust. I dwelled on the eye-for-an-eye, instead of the turning-the-other-cheek."

"It's not too late to start," Ruth said. "You're a young man still, Reese."

"Yeah, a young man who likely has rabies with a hurricane bearing down on him. Might just be too late."

Ruth took his hand. "I'm cold, Reese. Put your arms around me."

"You should go back to the fire."

"Put your arms around me, Reese."

Slowly, Reese stretched his arms out and draped them over Ruth's shoulders, entwining his fingers behind her neck.

"Pull me against your chest."

"You should go back to the fire."

"I need you, Reese. Not a fire. As you said, there's a big hurricane coming tomorrow."

Reese pulled Ruth against his chest, his breath quickening as Ruth put her arms around him. When she put her lips against his, he pulled back, but slowly he relaxed and let her kiss him. She smelled of smoke and salt. Her bosom was warm against his sore chest. Ruth pulled back an inch.

"Heal me, Reese. I'm scared. There's a hole right through my soul as big as a fist."

"I'm only human, Ruth. I can't heal."

"That's where you're wrong the most, Reese. Humans put the hole through me. Only a human can heal me."

Ruth rested her lips against Reese's neck. She inhaled, and he smelled of minerals and salts, so very different from the soaped and scented men she had been with.

"I wish I could heal," Reese said. Slowly he rotated his neck against Ruth's lips. "I wish I could go back in time and be on that radio when we were being tracked, and Brown was alive now with his family still wearing that cross I took from him. I wish I could walk through the hospital and lay my hands on people like Christ did and they'd be instantly healed."

"Christ did those things," Ruth admitted. "Wonderful things. But for every person he touched and cured, thousands of people still died every day. Life went on. He didn't come to the world to save it forever. He came to do the very best with every day he drew breath, so that at night when he was going to sleep he could say, 'Today I tried.' He came as a human. And when he left and rose into the clouds, he didn't tell his disciples the answers to healing and world peace. He said believe and do your best. You believe, Reese. And you're doing your best. I believe, and I'm doing my best. Sometimes we just use different words."

Ruth stood and helped Reese to his feet. She pulled her shirt over her head, then dropped her jeans to the sand and stepped out of them. Then — and without resistance — she unclothed Reese and pulled him against her. She pushed his hair back, then kissed him — gently at first, then harder as she felt him respond.

"Was that sinful?" she said, pulling back.

Reese smiled. "I didn't know it felt so good."

"What? Kissing?"

His face was already so red, the blush didn't show. "I never kissed a woman before. I've only been with a few prostitutes before I was saved, and they didn't ever kiss."

Ruth kissed Reese long and deep then, as they sank slowly to the sand. They used their senses, not their minds, and what they smelled, felt, tasted, touched, and saw became all of existence for those few minutes. They came at the same time, screaming together, and afterwards for a long while Ruth lay with her head against Reese's shoulder and cried while he stroked her hair.

"I'm all filled up. The hole is gone,"

Ruth finally said. She kissed Reese on the forehead, and went to warm herself by the fire. Reese sat looking over the water, which gleamed like a black pearl. "If I have sinned, Lord," he prayed, "please forgive me in the name of...." He stopped in mid-sentence. He didn't feel the urge, or, more importantly, the need to continue.

Chapter 9

Dawn was unusually quiet, the song-sters having taken wing, but bream and bass were still striking insects on the lake's surface. The sun crested the horizon in a blue sky without a hint of clouds. No wind stirred the branches.

Junuh was slow in getting up. Ruth and Reese were already doing chores before he finally came out from under the tattered piece of canvas he used as cover. He rubbed his face, staring into the fire, then over the water. "What train ran over me?" he finally asked.

"The grape train," Reese said with a chuckle. "The rot-gut grape train. Mashed you flat, Doc."

"I feel like it." Junuh coughed, then spit. "My head is splitting." He drew a circle around and around in the sand. "I didn't do anything I need to apologize about, did I?"

"Naw, naw," Reese answered.

"Don't worry about it," Ruth said. "I think the whole thing was very therapeutic for you."

"No, really," Junuh said with emphasis. "Several very unpleasant pieces of memory and words keep popping up in my head. Something about arguing over a chicken."

Reese stepped close to Junuh and extended his hand. He held his grip for several moments. "Seriously, Junuh. You got plastered on rot-gut wine and showed your butt a little bit. I can't remember how many times I did that before I got saved. Don't worry about it. You're a good man in my book."

"Yeah, Junuh," Ruth responded. "Don't worry about it. You needed to release some tension."

Reese dropped Junuh's hand. "I actually gained some new respect for you. A man that will tackle a jug of Richard's ain't scared of dragons."

"Well, seriously, if I said or did anything out of order, I'm sorry. Truly I am. I apologize. Something snapped in me last night that needed to come out. I just hope I didn't do anything to hurt your feelings or lose your respect. We've been through a lot the last few days."

Junuh heaved to his feet and walked down to the sandbar to relieve his bladder. He searched the lake for signs of a boat, but he saw only circles created by feeding fish and the far shoreline magnified on the lake's surface.

When Junuh returned, Ruth was humming. Reese was trying to find a radio station strong enough to be pulled in by the weak batteries. He and Ruth had kept a shy

distance all morning. Occasionally they held
eyes. Finally Reese's tuning drew a male voice
telling about the storm.

"The latest update has Hurricane Dena
rated as a strong category-four. Winds
around the eye are sustained at one-hundred-
forty-three miles an hour. The eye is expected
to pass over Cape Hatteras at mid-afternoon,
then follow a line that will take it just south
of Raleigh. The governor has already declared
a state of emergency with National Guard
troops activated...."

Reese turned off the radio as Junuh approached. "I have the right to hear, Reverend. You treat me like you did Nate. Is it as
bad as your face shows?"

"Ain't bad if you're a catfish. Not a
cloud in the sky, and the man says hundred-
and-forty-mile-an-hour winds are just hours
away. I don't think we should even try to
bushwhack out now. Just make our stand
here."

Reese's cheek was stretched tight,
shiny and red from swelling. The bite marks
oozed a milky liquid.

"We'll all go to paradise," Ruth said.
"I've settled the matter, and there need be
no more debate. Soon as Son shows up, we're
getting in that boat."

Reese kept his eyes on the radio. "He
may not show up again. I haven't exactly been
friendly to him."

"He'll come," Ruth said. "And all of us
are going with him. He's been in this swamp
a long time."

"The Lord is my shepherd, I shall not

want," Reese said.

"And he sent Son as his guiding lamb, bonehead. He's coming, and we're going."

During the next two hours, Junuh kept the fire going, adding green leaves occasionally to increase the smoke. They were late already in returning; both Junuh and Ruth had been scheduled to work that morning, and people knew where they had gone, that they should have returned the previous night. Junuh repeatedly scanned the lake for a boat. He thought he saw one once, but it turned out to be just a beaver cutting a wake across the water. Reese foraged for grapevines. He put them in a pile, and when he had enough, began to strip them of shoots and leaves. Ruth absorbed herself in her thoughts, sitting in the chair with the urn at her feet.

"What are you going to do, build a vine bridge across the lake?" Junuh asked Reese.

Reese shook his head.

"What are all the vines for?"

"Ropes," Reese said. "That hurricane comes, we can't get in that hole again. We'd drown. That big oak," he pointed, "I figure we can tie ourselves to the trunk."

"Sort of like the Ancient Mariner?"

"I don't know about any ancient mariner. I do know that hundred-and-forty-mile-an-hour winds can blow you away."

"Blow oak trees away, too."

Reese looked up sharply. "Not if God protects that tree." The clouds began to arrive from the northeast, at first high cirrus clouds that thickened slowly into a low, gray mass. The wind freshened, and now blew in the right direction to carry a man lying on a log across the lake.

Son came within the hour. He stepped from his boat with water draining from his feet, the leak apparently something he hadn't been able to fix. Ruth met him before he was halfway to the fire. She hugged him, the swamp man's arms hanging stiffly by his sides.

"I knew you would come. We're ready to go with you to paradise if the offer is still extended."

Son nodded. "*Genesis* 2:8: 'And the Lord God planted a garden eastward in Eden and there he put the man he had formed.'" He took a step back from Ruth. His eyes warmed and crinkled at the edges. He looked first into Ruth's eyes, then at her stomach and smiled. "*Genesis* 9:7: 'And you, be ye fruitful, and multiply; bring forth abundantly in the earth, and multiply therein.'"

Reese stopped stripping vines, jolted by the words; his face darkened for a moment like a white cloud before the sun. He held Ruth's eyes for several seconds, then beckoned to Junuh.

"You two grab your stuff and get in that boat. Get on out of here. That hurricane is only a few hours away."

"We're all going," Ruth said. "We've been together the whole time, Reese. We can't separate now. Especially now!"

Reese's jaw tightened. He looked across the water silently, his hands jammed into his trouser pockets. "Y'all go on. I'm staying, and nothing is going to change my mind. His boat wouldn't float us all, anyhow."

"We'll bail," Junuh said. "He said it's not far."

Reese said nothing for a long moment. "Look, I've made up my mind. I didn't sleep a wink last night. I have to stay here. You can't understand, I know, but I have to."

"You'll die here," Junuh said.

"And you might die there. But I have to follow my faith. I don't see God in this man. But, I might be wrong. I'll pray for you."

"Peter Matthiessen walked all the way to the Crystal Monastery," Son said. "But he didn't see a snow leopard because he looked too hard."

"Look, Swamp Man, you may be all right. There might be a Wal-Mart and a McDonald's a half mile from here, and you're just trying to take me there. But I see this as a test of my faith, and my faith is telling me to tie myself to that tree. I was the only guy to crawl out of a burning tank, and I didn't deserve it. Maybe in the next few hours, I'll understand why."

Ruth came to Reese and encircled him with her arms. She kissed him close to his ear. "Last night was..."

"Last night was the will of God," Reese said, cutting her off. "I have no problems with last night. He smiled and tightened his arms against her. Taking the cross from around his neck, he pressed it into Ruth's palm, but quickly his face went stern again. "And I have no problem with staying here — and I am."

Ruth kissed him again. She picked up

the urn and walked to Son's boat. Junuh followed. Water stood three inches deep inside.

"Go ahead and go with him, Ruth," Junuh said. "I think he's taking you someplace safe. Me, I'm staying here with Reese."

"That's suicide, Junuh."

"Maybe. But for the first time since becoming a grown man, I'm making a decision with my heart. You're right about some things. I think we were brought here for a reason. I'm a doctor, and if Reese survives this storm, he's going to need help getting out of here. He's already running a high fever. I can't leave a sick man." Junuh hugged her, then walked back to Reese.

"I know you're nuts now, Doc."

"Well, at least I'm something. I feel like I have a name now. Call me nutty, but I believe I'm supposed to stay here. I finally believe in something. Imagine that."

Ruth waved until they were well off shore, tears rolling down her face.

The creek was marked only by a break in the wind-damaged willows. The water was as dark as strong tea; cypress knees crowded the banks, the creek no wider than ten feet. Trees arched over it, creating the effect of a tunnel. Some had fallen into the water during the storm, and Son had to maneuver through them. Ruth felt a hint of fear, but took a deep breath and blew it away.

Is he going to cut my throat? Is this the River Styx? Am I going to look back at Son and see a skeleton poling? Am I passing through a door that will carry me into another time? Was Reese right all along?

Ruth's thoughts were as dark as the water on which she floated. She dispelled each with a deep cleansing breath. Paradise. I am on a boat floating to paradise. Goodness rules the universe, and Son is a man of goodness.

After about a quarter mile, the trees thinned; the sudden light seemed especially bright. A dock had been built into the water, and Son poled the boat into it at an angle. He stepped out, knotted a rope over a post, and reached an arm out to Ruth.

A beautiful log cabin sat beneath a large oak. The cabin was built of cypress, the logs peeled and notched at the corners like interlaced fingers. The roof was covered with hand-split shingles. Flowers filled rock-bordered beds, some of them flattened by the storm. Clipped grass grew between the flowerbeds; behind the house, Ruth could see the remains of a vegetable garden. Clearly, Son had been cleaning up after the storm. Piles of limbs lay at the edge of the woods, where she could see a few downed pines.

As Ruth was taking in all of this, she saw the sign, hand-painted on a piece of wood, written in calligraphy and nailed above the front door — PARADISE, the letters colored like a rainbow.

"Oh Toto," she whispered, "we're not in Kansas."

"Welcome," Son said. "Received gladly into one's presence or companionship."

"Thank you. I'm glad to be here. Did

you build the cabin, Son?"

He shook his head. "Merrie did."

"Merrie, she was your mother, wasn't she? Where is she now?"

Son beckoned with one hand. He led her to the base of a large magnolia tree. A frame of colorful rocks encircled a grave, and at the head of the grave stood a slab of soapstone with words engraved.

MERRIE MANN
A GOOD MOTHER
1943 - 1995

The letters had been painted with alternating colors. The mound of earth above the grave was covered with objects and artifacts from nature — unusually colorful stones, animal bones, turtle shells, pine cones, flowers and berries in various stages of drying, shed snake skins, oddly shaped sticks, the rack from a large deer, Indian arrow heads — things that had caught Son's eye over the years. It was apparent that these had been removed before the storm and carefully replaced afterward. The grave offered a sense of timelessness. Merrie Mann. So much of the mystery dissolved now. Ruth thought for a moment of trying to get back to Reese. If Reese came, Junuh would. But Ruth also felt an acute sense of destiny, of what was meant to be....

"You must have loved her very much. I bet you miss her."

"*John* 7:33: 'Yet a little while I am with you, and then I go unto him that sent me.'"

Son leaned over and picked up a pinch of dirt from the grave. "'Dust in the Wind,' Kansas." He sprinkled the dirt, his head cocked to one side while he sang, "Dust in the wind, All we are is dust in the wind."

Ruth watched him, so childlike one moment, but able to slit a fawn's throat the next. He seemed to live totally within the moment. He must have lived alone since his mother's death, surviving off lessons she had taught him.

The sky was getting darker, the wind picking up. The land where she stood was the highest Ruth had seen around the lake, so flooding probably wasn't a threat, but she wondered if the cabin would survive the winds to come. Son seemed to be reading her thoughts. He suddenly took her hand and led her behind the cabin. The air was filled with the notes of wind chimes; two homemade creations hanging from the back porch. Chickens in a wire pen clucked and scratched at the sight of the humans. A grassy knoll was behind the house, an iron pipe protruding from it. A path led to an arched entrance and twin metal doors on the ground's surface. Son lifted one of the doors, then the other. "Bob Dylan," he said. "Shelter from the storm."

He reached inside, flipped a switch, and suddenly the sunken room was filled with inviting battery-powered light. He invited Ruth to enter, and she hesitated only for a moment before following the steps down into the cool air. She was not surprised at the order and neatness she encountered.

The walls were of cinder blocks coated with concrete, painted white. Shelves along the walls held home-canned vegetables, fruits, stews, cooking utensils, a folded four-burner Coleman stove, a dozen gallon cans of cooking fuel. Military water canisters were stacked against one wall. There were books, too, even in this humid place, novels, a thick volume of Shakespeare's plays, and one titled *After: Surviving a Nuclear War,* all showing signs of mildew. Decks of cards, a backgammon board, a chess set were better protected, all still in plastic wrappers awaiting players. A dozen car batteries were stacked against one wall. Some sort of mechanical contraption sat close to the batteries, and from the looks of it, Ruth supposed it was a type of hand-operated generator. On a table was a citizen band radio as well as a conventional radio. Constructed against another wall were twin bunk beds, one atop the other, both mattresses neatly covered with sheets, blankets, and pillows. Ruth's worries about the storm melted. The house and trees might not stand up to the winds, but a shelter designed to withstand nuclear war surely would.

When Ruth looked back up at the entrance, Son was nowhere in sight. She climbed out and called to him, but only the chickens answered. She called again, but saw no sign of him. She hoped he had returned to get Reese and Junuh.

The cabin beckoned to her, seeming almost to call her name in the sounds of the wind. She didn't think Son would mind her entering. The front door was unlocked, the

cabin cool inside, the windows open. The fur-
nishings were simple and sturdy. Ruth was
drawn first to the photographs. They were
everywhere, some framed on the walls, others under a sheet of glass that topped a table.
A woman Ruth assumed to be Merrie was in
most of them. She had Son's blue eyes, the
exact shape and hue. She was pretty in a
woodsy, hippie way; her hair long and often
in braids. She wore dresses in most of the
photos, long and loose around her legs. She
was with Son in many, he at ages from infant
to manhood. Nearly all of the pictures had
been taken at the cabin. But a few, clustered
together, were from a city: a fountain shot,
several inside a home, Merrie holding onto a
black man roughly her age. He had to be Son's
father. The shape of his face, his overall build
were the same. Curiously, Ruth could find
no picture that placed mother, father and Son
together, none that linked the man to the
cabin.

Next, Ruth was drawn to the books.
Perhaps a thousand lined shelves along the
walls, fiction and non-fiction, many classics,
but a fair number of contemporary and
lighter themes. Many were on religion, the
Bible, the *Koran*, Eastern philosophies. Now
Ruth understood Son's ability to quote in
such range and accuracy. An old phonograph
occupied one corner of the room, powered
by a car battery. Ruth flipped through the
old albums and forty-fives: classical, blue-
grass, rock and roll, and jazz.

She must have been a brilliant woman,
Ruth thought. Such wide interests. She must

have worked very hard to educate Son in the ways that he could learn.

In another corner of the cabin was a desk with a manual typewriter, reference books, and stacks of paper. Taped to the typewriter was a letter. Ruth carefully removed it and held it up to read.

Dear Nurse R???,

You have come here finally, and I hope that my prayers are answered and that Micah is well and that the cabin and property are in good order. I knew from the visions I had that you would come eventually, and that you were a nurse, but I could never quite make out your name. I'm sorry.

I am dying of cancer and I know that my days are short. I have done my best to prepare Micah for the time when I will not be present in body, but he understands that I will be with him in other ways.

Micah and his paternal twin, Nathaniel, were born to me when I was twenty-two, only a year out of Harvard. Their father unfortunately did not live up to his end of the agreement. When Micah was less than two years old, I realized he was 'special.'

Unfortunately, due to my circumstances, which were not good, I was forced to make a hard choice. I chose Micah because I knew he was going to face a tough life due to his mental condition and, unlike Nathaniel, he clearly looked bi-racial. I pray that Nathaniel knows in his heart I was doing what I thought was best for him. I always had a deep feeling that he not only would do good for himself, but even more for others.

Despite the estrangement from my parents, I inherited these two-hundred acres of land that have been in the Mann family since before the Revolutionary War. I had never been comfortable in 'modern society' and knew that Micah would suffer from such an uncaring culture. I built this cabin when he was five. I called it Paradise because I hoped that here, cut off from a heartless modern world, my son and I could find happiness living close to God and Mother Earth.

I don't know why you have come here, but I hope that the events that brought you are turning out as they should. In my visions, I saw storms, but eventually a rainbow. I always knew that Micah being born 'special' was for an ultimate good that was bigger than us, and I believe that you are part of that plan.

Love and Peace,
Merrie Mann

Ruth was crying as she finished the letter. She held it to her bosom, swaying slightly from side to side. She closed her eyes, thinking back over the past few days, the incredible unlikeliness of all that had happened. She felt a warm presence surrounding her, as if arms were holding her tight. She stood that way until a clap of thunder brought her back into the real world. Following the boom, she heard Son calling her name. She found him with coils of rope looped over his shoulders. The sky was black, the wind beginning to make small trees lean.

"Sanctuary," he said. "A novel by Faulkner. A place of refuge and protection. You have to go there now, Ruth. The wind is coming."

A flash of lightning turned the world white. "Yes, I think we better get in the shelter now."

Son took her hand and led her there. "I have to go," he said. "I need to get there before the wind."

"Go where? You're getting into this shelter with me."

Son shook his head. "I have to be with them."

Ruth realized now what the rope around Son's shoulder was for. "You'll be killed just like them. Your mother worked hard for you. She had a plan."

"Plan: a method for achieving an end. Ruth, Paradise won't be the same after the hurricane. Neither will I. A method for achieving an end."

"You can rebuild Paradise. I'll help you."

197

Son laid his hand against Ruth's stomach. "*Matthew*, 20:28: 'And even as the Son of man came not to be ministered unto, but to minister, and to give his life as a ransom for many.'"

Son withdrew his hand. "I've dreamed of Nathaniel and the wind. McLaurin, *Cured by Fire*: 'All of life is one big wheel that takes us in circles.'"

Son turned and walked toward the dock. Ruth watched but did not speak. Lightning flashed again, and when her eyes cleared, Son had disappeared over the lip of the dock. She carried the urn into the shelter, and after placing it on a table, climbed back up to close and latch the heavy doors. The doors shut out most of the sounds of the approaching storm, and Ruth felt as if she were in a womb. She sat in a chair and began to weep.

Reese and Junuh debated the pros and cons of storms and trees before deciding to take their stand in a grove of small pines that grew on the highest spot on the island.

"Those big trees are coming down," Reese said. "That you can depend on. We'll just have to hope they don't fall on us. Maybe these pines will bend with the wind."

The two men hurriedly began weaving the grape vines into strands. The clouds had grown so thick that darkness seemed to be descending, the rain picking up hard and steady, with bursts of lightning and thunder every few seconds. Selecting two trees a few feet apart, they looped the vines around their bodies and the trunks, pulling the bindings tight.

"I've said some things I regret," Reese said. "You're a good doctor, Junuh. You did all you could for Nate. I know that."

"We've all said things in anger we didn't mean," Junuh responded. "I don't have any problems with you, Reese. You're a good man. The world would be better with more like you."

The rain was coming in sheets now, the wind beginning to roar.

"You been baptized, Junuh?" Reese asked, shouting over the wind.

He shook his head. "Mama wanted me to. I never did."

"About God. What do you believe?"

Junuh looked up at the dark sky. "I've learned some things in the last three days. I've changed in some ways. There's something bigger than me. Better than me. There's a plan, but it's still just too big for me to understand."

"Heck, do you think I understand it? That 'something' you mentioned. Could you call it God?"

Junuh nodded. "I could. I could do that."

Reese took off his cap and held it out. Rain poured into it. "Look at me," Reese said.

Junuh turned his head and looked directly into Reese's eyes, rain pouring across his face. Reese stretched to empty his cap over Junuh's head.

"I baptize you in the name of the Fa-

ther, and of the Son, and of the Holy Ghost."
He reached into his shirt pocket, took out a
small, soggy piece of the bread that Son had
brought them. Tearing it into two pieces, he
handed one to Junuh. "This here is commun-
ion. This bread is the flesh of Christ. Eat it."

Reese popped his into his mouth and
swallowed. Junuh did the same.

"Open your mouth and let some rain
hit your tongue. That's the blood of Christ."

Both men leaned their heads back and
let rain pour into their mouths, washing
down the bread.

"Son of a gun!" Reese roared. "It's
done, Junuh. Let the storms come and the
mighty waves roll. We stand here. We are
pure, and death can claim no vic-to-ry."

Reese raised his hands toward the sky.
"I don't understand it, Lord, and I don't particularly like lightning, but bring it on. Your
will be done, on Earth as it is in Heaven. Ju-
bilation, let it roar."

"Daddy would be proud of me," Junuh
said. "I think for the first time, he would be
proud of me."

"And he's looking on right now," Reese
said. "He sees you, Junuh, and he's proud to
have raised a man who will stand up to a
hurricane."

Reese saw Son then, almost an appari-
tion at first. He pointed toward the lake,
through the sheets of rain and the flashing
lightning at the figure walking knee-deep
along the shore toward them. They saw him
crossing the sandbar, his chest heaving from
exertion, the ropes coiled over his shoulder.

Son them then and veered toward them.

There was no talk, no need for it, each man in his own way understanding and accepting. Son handed a length of rope to Reese and Junuh, then backed against a tree between them, a short distance behind, and began to loop the rope until he was bound tightly. The men had barely finished when amid the noise of the storm arose a sound, as if Earth herself were in upheaval. Greater forces than they had ever known were enveloping them.

Chapter 10

From the sanctuary of the shelter, Ruth could hear the storm as it grew from whine to roar. She sat in a chair with the urn cradled in her lap, knowing that Reese, Junuh and Son were facing the full force of the storm. She prayed fervently for them.

Above her secure retreat, the rain blew thick and horizontal, almost like a river. Small trees bent to the wind, larger ones losing branches that on snapping floated for a moment, then swept in an arc to the ground, tumbling until stopped by solid objects. Shingles lifted one-by-one from the cabin's roof, disappearing into the sheet of rain. Lightning grew in frequency and intensity, a cosmic stroboscope.

The first tornado to pass close by was small but powerful enough to twist huge limbs from sturdy old oaks and cypresses. Ruth heard the funnel making its destructive way through the forest, growling like some prehistoric creature, and she gripped the urn tighter, glancing anxiously at the bolted latch that held the shelter's doors closed.

As the eye of the hurricane approached, the circle the wind followed tightened, and Ruth could hear the increased force as she continued to pray for the three men.

Shingles now flew from the cabin like a swarm of birds, and ancient trees exploded at the base and toppled in domino fashion. With the shingles gone, the wind began grabbing roof boards and ripping them away.

The fury abated rapidly as the eye approached. Within minutes, the roaring and banging stopped. An eerie silence ensued, and Ruth put down the urn, climbed to the door, and listened for a few moments before opening it. She saw clear blue sky, washed of every molecule of dust and pollen. But to her horror, she was surrounded by destruction. Only the thick, log walls of the cabin stood. Limbs and debris were everywhere. Most of the large trees had fallen, some with root balls much taller than she, leaving craters, now muddy pools, where they once had stood. One tree had smashed the chicken pen. Miraculously, some of the chickens survived. Ruth saw two casually pecking at the ground, as if nothing unusual had taken place. The huge magnolia shading Merrie's grave had been toppled, but had fallen away from the headstone. Ruth looked toward the lake, but caught only a glimpse of it through the fallen trees. The creek was roaring, and she knew that the island probably was flooded. She couldn't imagine what Reese, Junuh, and Son had endured and feared for them. Were they alive? Hurt? Had they found purpose in their ordeal?

Ruth's thoughts were interrupted by a distant roll of thunder. To the east, another line of ominous clouds was rapidly climbing the horizon as the second half of the storm approached. Ruth retreated again to the safety of the shelter, bolting the latch behind her.

The wind came from the opposite direction now, and some trees that had managed to lodge themselves half erect were now pushed back into the craters they had occupied. The creek crashed over the dock, splintering it, and ripping it from its moorings. The notched logs of the cabin walls yielded to a second tornado, this one much bigger than the first, snatching up the heavy logs and whirling them into the sky like sticks. This tornado, whirling ferociously within the harsh, bigger circle, was clearing a path hundreds of feet wide through the forest.

As it approached, Ruth huddled against a wall in the concrete womb, the urn between her knees. The sound was deafening, and the very earth was vibrating. Ruth wondered if even this shelter could protect her. She closed her eyes, praying hard, and when she opened them she saw Nate in the dim light of the lamp. The vision brought an immediate memory of him drawing circles on a pad in his hospital bed. And Ruth heard his voice as clearly now as then, "Inside the circle, I will return to you."

She understood then, realized what Nate had been trying to tell her, and what had come true. She rose and climbed the stairs to the shelter doors, the noise now overwhelming. The doors shuddered.

Ruth crouched on the open steps, hooking her legs around them. She struggled with the bolt and slid it open. Both doors sprang outward.

Fish were raining from the sky. Small silver fish and larger, darker ones. They flapped against the ground and continued to fall. The tornado wall, nearly translucent, was passing overhead. Ruth saw whole trees and sheets of roofing tin from the chicken house swirling in it. Her hair stood straight up. Light objects inside the shelter, freed from gravity, zipped past her as she fought to stay rooted on the stairs. She stared with awe into the tornado's vortex, a long, curved tube, luminous at the far end deep inside clouds. She lifted the urn with both arms outstretched. The cap was instantly sucked off, and a plume of Nate's ashes danced, twirling toward the brightness at the top of the funnel. The ashes gushed forth in a flash, and the urn, too, was snatched from Ruth's hands and tumbled out of sight.

A shadow engulfed Ruth as the vortex passed and the racing wall of rain reappeared. The tornado became darker as it crashed on through the forest, devouring trees. One of the shelter doors slammed shut as the funnel moved on, and It took all of Ruth's strength to close the other and reset the bolt. She fell into the chair, her energy spent, and soon drifted into sleep as the storm continued to rage.

While Ruth dozed, the hurricane passed, its departure much quicker than its approach. She awakened to silence. Slowly she climbed the stairs and pushed open the twin doors, letting them fall against the earthen roof of the shelter. She gazed into a world of utter destruction. Little was recognizable. The cabin was gone, the forest nearly flattened. No part of Paradise was left untouched. Even Merrie's headstone had been snatched away. Ruth could see the swollen lake, which now reached much farther inland. The water was brown and beginning to calm. She could see the island where she, Reese and Junuh had camped, but it was inundated, the treeline broken, and she knew in her heart that none of the three men could have survived. She collapsed, sobbing, to the sodden earth, and remained there while the sun dropped and burned a red stripe from shore to shore across the lake.

The butterflies came then, four of them. They alighted on her shoulders and hair, wings folding and unfolding as they rested. Ruth knew instinctively that they had come with a purpose and was careful not to disturb them. One crawled across her forehead, its feet tickling her skin. They left as suddenly as they came, taking wing in a swirl toward the setting sun.

Ruth's hand went to her belly. She sensed a special warmness there, a vibration of life that increased as cell begat cell. She felt a calmness and peace she never had known. No urgency pressed her. Amidst destruction, chaos and sorrow, the buried shelter offered order, light, food, water, books, a dry, warm bed, the promise of strength. In a day or two she would walk out of this wilderness and find people. She wouldn't try to explain anything because no one would understand. Nobody else needed to understand.

Epilogue

Outside the weather-grayed farmhouse, an eastern breeze tinkled the garden wind chime. The young farmer and his wife talked little over breakfast of eggs, ham, and hot coffee that bled steam into the air.

"The weatherman said that some places could expect five or six inches," the woman said. She carefully cut a tiny piece of ham. "That's a lot."

"Yeah, it is. We'll just have to wait and see. We need the rain. God, we need it."

Early afternoon, and the farmer was atop his tractor, gazing at the blush of winter wheat that tinted the gray soil. Beyond the field, the earth swelled to the western slopes of the Appalachians. He watched with growing excitement as dark, rolling clouds from the spent hurricane spilled over the blue-green mountains.

The first rain drops were huge and splatted against the dry soil. The vanguard thickened into a steady rain that brought the wife into the yard where she stood waving at her husband across the field.

That night she and her husband lay entwined in bed, the drum of rain against the tin roof as steady as the innocent sleep breath of her husband. The woman knew their good fortune was at the expense of others, that people along the coast had lost homes to the storm — that lives, too, had been taken. But in her own domain, the fragile wheat would grow. They would make a harvest, and that wheat would feed many. The bank collector would stay away, and in the spring, she would plant flowers and early vegetables as soon as the frost allowed. She fell to sleep in thanksgiving, knowing a life lived through faith in goodness should harbor no fear or shame.

Acknowledgments

The publication of this book was made
possible through the hearts and hands of the
following people: Erik Bledsoe, Jerry Bledsoe,
Larry Brown, Clyde Edgerton, Laura Guy, Phil Jones,
Bruce McLaurin, Carol McLaurin, Jake Mills,
Beth Hennington and Lee Smith.

Erik Bledsoe: Herculean editing.
Jerry Bledsoe: Herculean editing.
Larry Brown: blurb and feedback letter,
encouragement.
Clyde Edgerton: blurb, feedback, proofing and
printing the original manuscript,
shipping it to Stella, etc, encouragement.
Laura Guy: retyping original core manuscript
into a format for Tim's new laptop.
Phil Jones: computer repair assistance.
Bruce McLaurin: gift of laptop to Tim allowing
him to write from couch, hospitals, etc.
Carol McLaurin: tried to keep author alive.
Jake Mills: feedback letter, editing,
encouragement.
Beth Hennington: booksetting.
Lee Smith: blurb, feedback letter,
encouragement.

Carol McLaurin

DATE DUE

NOV 1 7 2004	
DEC 1 8 2004	
JAN - 5 2005	
JAN 2 6 2005	
FEB 1 1 2005	
FEB 1 1 2005	
FEB 1 6 2005	
FEB 2 6 2005	
MAR - 8 2005	
MAR 3 1 2005	

GAYLORD   PRINTED IN U.S.A.